Calf Love

Joyce Fussey

Robson Books

Dear Wards and Lewises.
This one is for you, with all my love.

First published in Great Britain in hardback in 1984 by
Robson Books Ltd, Bolsover House, 5-6 Clipstone Street,
London W1P 7EB. This Robson paperback edition first
published in 1987.

Copyright © 1984 Joyce Fussey

British Library Cataloguing in Publication Data

Fussey, Joyce
   Calf love.
   1. North York Moors (England)—Social
   life and customs
   I. Title
   942.8'460858'0924   DA670.Y6

   ISBN 0-86051-426-9

Printed in Great Britain by Biddles Ltd., Guildford.

Contents

1

Who's for hemlock?

To take the charitable view, I blame my husband Gordon's mental lapse on brain damage due to innumerable encounters between his head and our low doorways, beams and the bathroom ceiling.

Didn't he once—forgetting that the bath nestles under the eaves—attempt to stand up, crack his head on the sloping ceiling and pitch headlong over the side of the tub with a foundation-shaking crash which drew the family from points as far away as the farmyard? Obviously, these blows did him no good and are, I stoutly maintain, the sole reason why he fenced the boundaries of the calf field with wood cut from the sawn-down yew tree.

The outcome proved that he had not been so misguided as we thought at the time but, even so, something more conventional . . . a run of good oak posts, say, or even a bit of split chestnut paling would not have landed me in the sort of situation which, merely to think about now, makes my hair stand on end.

The first part of that day was uneventful . . . even pleasant. I ought to have recognized it as the beginning of that joke which fate plays on us (the one where she almost persuades us that things are going right for once, then the minute we drop our guard she wades in and lets us have it) when there was no chaos in the cowhouse and all was calm

5

in the calfpens. Even more significant, the morning's baking went like a dream without a single pie losing its top in the Rayburn and hardly a bun dropped in the ashes. The pies, bursting with apples of our own growing that had wintered aromatically in the attic, both looked and smelled good as they cooled on racks in the kitchen. I can't *think* why I didn't catch on.

After lunch young Roger and I visited friends who lived in the cottage at Ghyll House Farm. Mary's second baby was due to be born on the following day and we admired the pretty cot and layette created by Mary's clever fingers. In the gathering dusk of the January afternoon we left the narrow road and hurried back at Scout's pace along the tractor track which drops down the moor to the fields edging the beck. It was clement for the time of the year and we actually sang aloud as we crossed the high, narrow footbridge spanning the ever-active, luminous water. Roger ran indoors to where my mother and a cheerful fire waited but I, making use of daylight's scant remains, went on into the farmyard and the outbuilding known as the doghouse, where the cattlefood was kept.

Euphoria surrounded me like a nimbus as I scooped cattle-rearing nuts and rolled barley into the calves' feed buckets and sprinkled spicy-smelling powdered minerals over it. The smell reminded me of the apple pies beckoning from the kitchen and dwelling happily on those I jostled through the reception commitee inside the calf field and raced it to the feeding troughs inside the hut. To a backing of appreciative chomps and slurps I stood outside for a moment savouring the evening and vaguely wondering about the strange, light stripes standing out from the dark perimeter of the field. Only for a second I wondered, for that was the moment Providence pulled the rug out from under.

Every one of those yew-wood fence posts had been stripped clean of bark.

Don't think I wasn't used to the sensation of my heart plummeting into my boots. After four years at Westwath it had practically grafted itself to my toes. I kicked it aside and tottered over to the first post. My momentary wild hope that owing to some magnetic pull of nature the bark had merely fallen off, was dashed to the ground. The branch's pinky-grey underskin was gouged in several places by the strong wide teeth of cattle.

I examined the next post. It, too, had been stripped to the buff. And the next and all of them apart from a few at the farther end which weren't made from yew but cut from harmless bird-cherry.

The animals were still inside the hut chasing fugitive calf-nuts around the bottom of the troughs. I dragged the door shut, shot home the bolts and pelted for the telephone and our hot line to the vet.

'*Yew* bark!' After the first startled exclamation at the other end of the line there followed a short silence during which the last vestige of hope drained away. His next words did nothing to renew it.

'Oh dear,' he said, 'I think you may be in trouble.' It was our regular vet's new assistant and he had yet to learn that we were *always* in trouble. 'Hold on a minute. I'm looking through the poison book.'

I could faintly hear pages flipping over and his voice muttering, 'Yew... yew. Yes, here we are. Yew *leaves*... mm . . . yew *twigs*. You did say, bark? Not leaves or twigs? Bark doesn't appear to be mentioned here.'

'Bark, yes. Off branches. *Dead* branches,' I qualified, clutching desperately at straws.

'Hmm,' said the vet, 'it says here that dead yew is more lethal than fresh. Though how,' he debated heatedly, 'they can say that I don't know because lethal is lethal, isn't it? And yew poison is like cyanide—practically instantaneous. You can't get more lethal than that, can you?'

My knees gave way. I clung to the phone for support.

'In fact . . .' he paused. 'You are sure the calves were OK when you left them?'

'I th-think so,' I stammered. 'They were eating their tea.'

'Seems to me, then, they stand a very good chance. Got

any liquid paraffin?'

'A few ounces,' I said, mentally reviewing the contents of the sideboard cupboard.

'That's no good. They'll need at least half a pint each. How many are there? Five of them. OK, I'll be there in twenty minutes.'

And so he was. (Because I had caught him right at the beginning of surgery, he left, we later discovered, a waiting-room full of disgruntled people and pets.) Between us we poured half a pint of liquid paraffin down each throat.

'Keep them in and watch 'em, but they should be all right.' He shone his torch over the half door and peered inside for a long time. 'I think,' he said.

'We'll get those posts out tomorrow,' I promised, as we crossed the field together.

'I shouldn't bother. They've eaten off the bark but they can't eat the wood. If I were you, I'd just paint them over with creosote or bitumen. That'll keep them off.' As I remarked before, he didn't know us—or our stock—very well.

Next day I was too scared to go to the calf field. Gordon (it was Saturday, so he hadn't gone to work) took the calf nuts instead, and came back reporting that everyone was as fit as a fiddle but, by gum, there wasn't half a mess inside the hut. Helped by our eldest son, twelve-year-old Robert, he spent the morning brushing bitumen thickly over each fence post.

There, he said confidently, when they had finished. That would cap the blighters. Which—incredibly, when you think about it—showed how little *he* knew us, also.

While he was at it, he said, he would do something about the quagmire outside the calf hut door. In this part of the country small springs of water tend to appear in unexpected places and one had recently bubbled up just where twenty hooves regularly trampled.

It would be somewhere to dump all that rubble, he said.

Rubble was something we had in plenty at that time. A

damp-course had been let into the house, a new roof put on and windows and doors broken into the walls. Mountains of broken stone, tiles and plaster stood slummily in the garden. By the end of that short winter's afternoon much of it had been transferred to the calf field, tipped into the mire and trampled down to make a firm entry into the hut.

'What did the calves make of the bitumen?' I asked, as Gordon kicked off his boots.

'Never looked at it,' he said positively as he gratefully accepted a mug of tea.

They didn't look at it the next day, either.

On Monday Gordon departed on his thirty-odd-mile journey to work, Robert and his younger brother, Antony, set off for school and I carried an armful of hay to the calf field.

They had looked at it by then all right. Every one of those dratted yew posts had been stripped again. Bitumen and all.

The calves gathered around me expectantly. They *had* enjoyed that nice liquorice stuff. Did I have any more? They hung around hopefully.

I stared at them helplessly. It wasn't as if they were hungry. All our animals were overfed as our neighbour, Will Arrowsmith, regularly told me. 'Ower fresh,' he said they were.

I tripped over my heart again as I anxiously wondered about bitumen. Was it poisonous? I had dialled half the vet's number before I remembered it was he who had suggested the stuff in the first place so it must be all right... But then, he hadn't expected them to *eat* it, had he..?

When we first moved out from Hull to this smallholding on the Yorkshire Moors a town friend remarked, 'But whatever will you find to *do*? Nothing ever happens in the country.' It is a phrase that springs to mind at least twice every day. I thought of it then and laughed hollowly.

Indecisively I returned to the field. Perhaps things were not so bad as I thought. Why I keep having these little surges of optimism it is difficult to understand.

Nothing had improved. Caroline, one of the heifers, had found a bit of liquorice that had been overlooked and was happily working on it. She was watched enviously by the others.

I went berzerk. 'You silly old bat,' I screamed. 'Get off it!' I shoved her, I smacked her, I biffed her. She lapped a long grey tongue round to the farther side of the post, put her head on one side and threw me a blissful, slant-eyed look. I belaboured her with a stick and she put her ears back enquiringly.

Then I had a bright idea—I stuck the stick in a cowpat and daubed it over the post.

As I hoped, Caroline stepped back fastidiously. My heart settled back into position with a sigh of relief. I circled the field painting each post with manure; five reproachful beasts following on my heels.

I returned to the house cheerful in the knowledge that I could now safely forget them until Gordon came home when he would, as he invariably did, conjure up a remedy. Initiative and ingenuity made up a great part of his character which, under the circumstances, was just as well.

An hour later I was fervently wishing that some of it had rubbed off on me. That was when I noticed that the morning's heavy mist had turned to pouring rain. Guessing the worst, I rushed round to the calf field. The beasts were clustered around a clean washed post. They turned contented heads to look at me. Wasn't it lucky, they said, about the rain..?

Something to take their minds off the posts ... but what? Organized games? A spelling bee? I-spy? I chopped up some turnips into a bucket and stuck it in front of their noses.

Back at the house I put my head in my hands and prayed for inspiration. The radio was imparting the news that a dangerous prisoner had escaped from gaol and was believed to be making his way over the moors to the Middlesbrough area. That was all I needed—everything astray always landed up here. I wondered if he would be any good at fencing..?

I could *not*, on my own, face the task of prising off the netting and barbed wire, digging out fence posts, cutting fresh ones from something that was not yew, putting them in and replacing the wire and netting. Then I had my second brilliant idea.

Next to the heap of rubble in the garden was a secondary pile of dry-rot-ridden wood which had been our skirting-boards. I picked up some lengths of the wood, filled my pockets with staples, hung a skein of binder-twine around my neck, collected a hammer and traipsed once more to the calf field. I faced each and every post with a piece of skirting-board, nailing it on where possible, tying with binder-twine where the gnarled posts bent away too far from the flat boarding. The calves accompanied me and helped by fraying out the twine and chewing the handle of the hammer each time I laid it down. When I picked up the hammer for the last time and started to leave the field they turned their attention to the skirting-boards and licked them tentatively.

And then it hit me what I had done. *I'd nailed every one of those blasted boards paint side outwards and had sentenced the stupid animals to die of lead poisoning.*

The rain poured down remorselessly. I was soaked to the skin and trickles tickled my shoulder blades. Mud caked my boots so that they were almost too heavy to lift. The leaden sky rested on leafless dejected trees and between it and me a small plane circled the field.

I realized now that, though until then unseen, its monotonous drone had been playing on my tight-strung nerves for some time. I waved the hammer at it in pure hate... then remembered the escaped prisoner. It was a search plane.

I moved out into the field to let myself be identified, futilely yelling that it was all right! It was only me!

The plane zoomed low over my head. I clapped my hands over my ears and brained myself with the hammer. The planed circled away.

Tears and rain mingled together as I dragged myself round that field again tearing off the boards, reversing them and nailing them back once more. I was nearly beside myself—though not as nearly beside as I was a minute later. The last bit of yew and lead safely concealed I plodded wearily towards the gate, turning there to throv a last malevolent glare at the animals.

Heads close to the ground they were in a furtive-looking bunch before the door of their hut. Warily I approached them.

They were picking out and eating something from the plaster rubble with which Gordon had cured the quagmire. It was tiny bits of paper. Bits of wallpaper. Green Edwardian wallpaper of the type which contained arsenic.

They suffered no ill effects at all but throve exceedingly.

They were beef cattle. I often wonder what happened to the consumers.

2

There is always a doctor in the house

After four years at Westwath we had given up expecting anything in the way of peace or tranquillity. The townsman's idyllic concept of country life—all that standing and staring—is a myth. No one has time for such things. In the event that a farmer *should* be observed standing and staring it is either because he is transfixed with rage at the sight of forty-two ramblers rambling forty-two abreast through his barley or else he has simply sunk immobilized into a bog. Nor is it likely he'll be leaning on a gate chewing a straw. For one thing, if his gates are anything like ours—and many of them are—a heavy lean would finish them off; and for another, straw costs money.

Since the moment our smallholding took us over we had hardly ever touched ground. Clocks stopped not because—as town-based friends tell us—in the country time is of no importance, but because we had been too busy to wind them up. We came to farming innocent tyros, learning the hard way by trial and—more particulary—error. Because the place was too small to support a family of six, Gordon got a job elsewhere and I, launched at the deep end and hindered by a crew of idiosyncratic animals led by a flock of mutinous sheep, fought madly to keep it afloat. The sheep had gone, but to our great surprise things were no better—cows, calves, cats, hens and even Jess, our beloved erstwhile sheepdog, did their darnedest to capsize us.

Though fairly waterlogged—to belabour this nautical metaphor I seem to have got stuck with—we were still on course and even making a little headway.

Gordon had bought a second-hand generator and, that February, laid down the foundations for an electricity supply to Westwath.

The foundations were literal and concrete. The site he chose for the generator house was underneath a raised outbuilding known as the Robin's Nest and there—after lifting a number of paving stones and discovering one of them to be a stone trough turned upside-down (instantly appropriated by me for the garden)—Gordon dug a hole which eventually received a one metre cube of concrete. And that is a lot more concrete than it sounds.

One good thing—most of the ingredients for it were near at hand. Sand, for instance, we quarried out of the man-high cliff which rises behind the house. The cliff supports the main hayfield and had, at some time long ago, been the bank of the beck. Over the years the beck had changed its course and now winds around the perimeter of the garden; our house standing on the actual rocky bed where once water swirled. The beck itself is a good source of gravel. We shovelled up the stones and riddled them through an old wire mattress. Cement—to our resentment—we had to buy.

In due course, the generator was set into its bed and, innocently unaware that years would pass before we could afford the next step, that of wiring up the house, we felt things were improving at last.

They weren't, of course. All in all it was to prove quite a year.

Before the month was out, Mother, then in her late seventies, became ill with Ménière's disease, an infection of the middle ear which causes sickness and extreme giddiness. The first to know about it—other than

14

Mother—was Antony who, sitting there inoffensively chuckling over an *Asterix* book, was knocked silly when the sky suddenly dropped on his head. That's what he thought it was, he complained later, but actually it was his grandmother who had suddenly keeled over and collapsed on top of him.

As was inevitable, Doctor Scott came at the same moment that the vet arrived to do the bi-annual TB test on the cows and heifers and each of them brought a companion—both distinctive in their own way. Crowded into our small kitchen we presented a typical Westwath tableau—surrealistic and fraught with symbolism.

In the centre as befits the chief character, Mother slumped sideways in a chair, bucket conveniently alongside, the rest of us crowded around her.

There was I anxiously describing her symptoms to the doctor while at the same time trying to give details of our herd to the vet. There was the doctor dividing his attention almost equally between Mother, me and the vet's wife who, judging by her size and shape, was even more imminently in need of his professional services than Mother was. There was the doctor's student assistant who, we understood, had come along for the experience, staring as if hypnotized at the kitchen sink wherein, deliberately and imperturbably, a cat sat under a dripping tap. And there was the vet, vet's wife, Mother and myself goggling at *him*, a creature so excessively clothed with hair from his shoulder-length mane and chest-covering beard down to the hem of an ankle-length musquash coat that *he* looked like a case for the vet.

Three days later the same company gathered again when Dr Scott paid another visit to Mother and the vet (the same, incidentally, who had been involved in the great calf poisoning affair; we had learned that his name was Cardew and he was beginning to learn one or two things about *us*) came to complete the second part of the TB test. Although we didn't know it at the time, the pattern was set for the year.

15

But we were only on the threshold of March with much to occupy us.

'What's the weather like up there in Injun country?' our butcher used to ask when we phoned in our weekly order. Aware that he would shortly have to brave it—whatever it was—he really wanted to know.

Here in the wild environment of the North Yorkshire Moors the weather high-handedly disregards the calendar and, in our own special realm of Westwath set in a bowl-shaped depression in the hills, flouts it altogether. We have known hard frosts in every month of the year including the so-called high summer ones of July and August. They slide down from the heights, by-passing the garden of our nearest neighbours, Binnie and Steven Brown (*their* rosemary bush isn't annihilated every single year, is it?), and settle happily on our marrow plants. Snow lying on our garden remains frozen there when the last vestige has melted away from everywhere else this side of Spitzbergen.

On the other hand, when the wind howls over the moor and bracken cringes and hunchback rowans bow their heads in submission; when walkers are brought to a standstill with eardrums battered and deafened; when drivers wrench at steering wheels to keep vehicles on the road, and Joan Arrowsmith's washing dries like a dream but is last seen heading at increasing altitude towards the next village—then we in our valley are sheltered and snug. And I bring in my limply-hanging washing to flap wetly about our ears in the kitchen.

Unless—quite a different story—the wind becomes trapped between the hills and is channelled along the beck, as it was only a few days after we had moved out from the city.

I was awakened that morning by what I thought were jungle noises. Tigers breakfasting on elephants. Or it could have been the other way round. Wide-eyed I peered through the window. There were cattle grazing the steep rough field on the opposite side of the beck—quiet-

16

appearing, placid creatures. One of these raised its soulful eyes and gazed dreamily into the distance. I should have like to have stroked its nose. Then, this gentle beast, without changing expression or giving any warning whatever, let off a sequence of deafening, blood-curdling cries that froze me to the spot. Eleven of these bellows there were, after which, no doubt feeling better for getting that lot out of its system, the cow resumed its grazing as if nothing had happened.

Unnerved, I continued looking through the window and that was when I became aware of the second remarkable sound. It was, I thought in my heightened state of tension, an express train tearing towards me down the valley. This puzzled me because I was pretty sure there were no railway lines down there. Though I wouldn't have sworn to it. We had barely lived in the place a week but already I could believe anything.

I pressed my cheek to the windowpane and squinted upsteam. On the edge of my vision the topmost branches of the alders and ashes began to quiver. The shudder ran downwards and the heavy lower limbs rose ponderously and fell again. The noise increased as neighbouring trees took up the baton; branches waved and threshed with increasing vigour until the whole valley was transformed into a Bedlam of sylvan dementia. Startling it was.

The postman was more than startled when, on another more recent occurrence of valley-funnelled wind, a tall tree snapped off halfway down its trunk, missing him by inches just as he was about to step on to our footbridge. He was shaking harder than the trees as he stumbled white-faced into our kitchen. It was hardly blowing at all up on top, he said, when his vocal chords were functioning again.

The first day of March began like that and by teatime even my endless lines of washing were dry enough for ironing.

Daffodils spiked the garden like tank traps and birds were much in evidence. Spring was so close I could smell her talc as I gathered in armfuls of fresh-air-filled sheets. I scanned the sky with a practised eye. Tomorrow would be another sunny, blowy day. I would wash a few blankets and, maybe, a quilt or two, I promised myself.

I should have done, too, if next morning there hadn't been three inches of snow on the ground and more coming down like a curtain. The snow was still there a week later when Mr Willis, the Man from the Ministry of Agriculture, came to inspect the calves.

This was an annual event and before setting foot on the farm the inspector always disinfected his boots in a bucket of water which I set at the gate for that purpose. The snow was frozen and compacted in well-trampled places like doorways and around the yard water-tap where I went to fill the bucket.

That was my first mistake because I could have filled it from the beck and had a shorter distance to carry it. The tap was stiff with cold which was the basis of my second mistake—I ought not to have tried to force it. The next second I was doing a spirited imitation of those little ping-pong balls that bob about on jets of water in shooting galleries, the broken-away tap still clutched in my hand.

Full in the face I caught all the pressure derived from the benefit of a long steep drop from the reservoir—a tank sunk in our neighbour's field way above the forest. I was paralysed witless for ages and when my brain did start up again its batteries were flat. All it came up with was that I should run up the road after Gordon who had left for work more than an hour ago.

Reluctantly dismissing that, I tried to ram the tap on again. The shape and range of the jet changed capriciously, soaring plume-like to the heights, spiralling helically, falling back in feathered parabolas—even in the state I was in I could imagine what *son et lumière* could do with it—but whatever form it achieved it always came down, icily, on me.

The stop-tap was buried unlocatably under the frozen snow—where else?—but my batteries were warming up a little now and the little grey cells were going into action. I reasoned that if all the other cold water taps on the property were turned on the pressure at this one would be reduced and I could then fit the tap back in place with no more ado.

I turned on the water in the cowhouse—mopping, while I was there, all my exposed parts with the old towel kept for the cows' udders—opened the tap in the doghouse, the one away round in the calf field and three in the house. While in the bathroom I changed all my clothes down to the skin.

I needn't have bothered with any of that. The fact I had overlooked was that the yard tap was at the lowest point of the whole system so the pressure was diminished not one whit, and when I tried once more to jam the tap back on to the pipe I got drenched again because I hadn't thought to turn the thing *on* first.

I won in the end—sort of—hoped I should remember not to be the first person to use the tap afterwards, and dashed to turn off all the others. By the time I got round to the calf field there was a flood around that one as well.

The calves, needless to say, were standing in a mesmerized group watching it. It fascinated them so much that it was ten minutes and a couple of pounds of calf-nuts later before they were enticed into their hut for the inspection. Mr Willis arrived, after washing his boots in beck water after all, and carefully weighed up the animals.

Afterwards while the calves shook their heads and expressed their surprise at having their ears punched like bus tickets, Mr Willis took out his tobacco pouch and seemed disposed to chat. How, he asked, had we fared with that Angus steer we'd had the previous year?

I knew whom he meant—Sidney, Rosie's fine upstanding son. We had been very proud of him and so were most disappointed when the price he brought at market was only average. But I was startled that Mr Willis, who had hundreds of calves pass through his hands each year, should remember him.

'Exceptionally good beast, that was,' Mr Willis's eyes glazed reminiscently. 'Best beast I've ever seen. In fact . . .'

19

his eye brightened, 'if I see a better beast than that I'll retire. There!'

With a friendly nod he departed leaving me with very mixed feelings and five calves huffily complaining that they, too, could have a figure like Sydney if they were given something to eat. What about extra hay rations all round?

3

Hatch and dispatch

March went out with a dying gasp that was just sufficient to make the gorse burn well without actually getting out of hand. To guard against the risk of uncontrolled fire, burning off is limited to the months between and including October and March and, every year, March jumps out on us before we know where we are. The gorse bushes do the same thing. We hack them to the ground, destroy the lot in a glorious crackling blaze then suddenly at the end of March there they are again marching in full armour up the Scar field from their briefing post on the roadside bank.

The annual fire ritual having been observed we turned expectantly to April. The month began joyfully with a christening when I stood as godmother to little Tracey Stewart, baby daughter of Mary and Joe of Ghyll House Farm.

We had a new baby at Westwath too. A four-legged one, younger brother to the legendary Sydney, and whose mother, Rosie, had tossed him into the world with so much vigour that he had flown past Rhoda in the neighbouring standing and landed in the dung channel immediately under Bluebell's tail.

I had noticed the ominous signs that afternoon when I staggered into the cowhouse beneath the herd's light lunch. She had had an udder like an inflated beachball for days but now there were further symptoms. Earnestly I pressed the hollows at either side of her tail to 'see if the strings had gone'. I did this because it's something farmers do though how it should feel when the strings had gone I didn't have a clue. After fifteen years I still haven't but continue to go through the motions.

It was still too early in the year for the cows to go out to the fields so I set about turning the cowhouse into a maternity ward. I swilled the floor for the umpteenth time then covered the whole surface with a thick layer of straw which the cows, feeling peckish again, cleared up to a radius corresponding with the limit of their neck chains.

Opposite, the calfpen was already prepared and waiting, walls scrubbed and whitewashed and a thick soft bed of shaken-out straw laid there, too. I remembered to rehang the half-door which Gordon had repaired and had scrubbed and scalded a small bucket for the new baby's feed.

There was even a pail of bran requiring only the addition of hot water to make the ante-natal warm bran mash without which none of the cows would dream of having a calf at all. There were clean sacks warming by the Rayburn and apart from gauze masks and scrubbing-up you couldn't have found a better-prepared midwife in the length and breadth of England.

Or a more reluctant one.

Oddly enough, every one of our previous calvings had taken place when Gordon had been conveniently in the offing. This time he wasn't, and I was worried to death. Not, as it turned out, without good reason. When at teatime Rose summoned me to the scene with an emotion-charged bellow, I opened the door and tumbled over the calf where he had landed just inside it (had it been open at the time I reckon he would have sailed across the yard and fetched up in the hayshed). On closer inspection I found he hadn't yet drawn a breath, and as he lay there, black and wet with his head at a funny angle, my own heart nearly stopped as well.

Feeling not the slightest bit like James Herriot and with my heart pounding away to make up for the beats it had missed I turned the head to a more natural position and with my free hand scooped thick yellow mucous out of the mouth and nostrils, willing life into him for all I was worth. At last, just as Robert, wide-eyed with excitement dashed up with the warm sacks, the calf sneezed explosively, its lungs expanded and contracted in an encouraging fashion and we both decided to live.

That, though, seemed as far as the calf was prepared to go. For ages he lay like an outsize beanbag while Robert and I, one at either end, scrubbed him with the sacks to dry him off and stimulate circulation, praying all the time that Bluebell, who was doubled round like a horse-shoe and pop-eyed with excitement for all she had seen dozens of calves in her time and was not a bit maternal anyway, wouldn't hop backwards on top of him.

When at length he did unwillingly scramble to his feet he found it was hardly worth the bother because his mother, side-stepping like Victor Sylvester, explained that baby minding wasn't her scene and why didn't he go and live with Will, next door. If someone hadn't shut the door before he was born, she pointed out reasonably, he would have been half way there already.

Hopefully I pushed the calf's nose to the udder and Rosie hopped about like a hysterical woman frightened of a mouse. If there had been a table handy she would have jumped on to it. It was the same every year. Neither Rosie nor Bluebell would ever suckle her young. Rhoda, on the other hand, would adopt all and everybody's.

Each year we tried, though. We edged the calf forward again, Robert shoving at its rear; me straddling it partly to support it with my knees, partly to be in a good position to push the teat into its mouth. The teat stretched like elastic as Rosie jumped up and down, the calf, utterly fed up, said he didn't want it anyway and I wished we had stayed in Hull and bred canaries.

We gave up then, Robert and I, and half-pushed, half-carried the hefty young bull to his nursery across the yard. I milked some sticky, colostrum-filled fluid from an udder that startlingly resembled those inflated Space-hoppers that were all the rage with children a few years ago, and told the calf to swallow it or else.

Satisfied that he would now have some internal protection from infection I let him get on with sleeping the sleep of the innocent which was something I should have given a lot to be doing myself.

But I hadn't finished yet. There was still the cleansing (afterbirth) to come and be disposed of. With gruesome memories of a previous occasion when I had had to gather up the disgusting thing by hand I thrust a large bucket into Robert's unwilling arms, stationed him behind Rosie's rump and told him to catch the cleansing as it was expelled. He needn't worry, I assured him. There was absolutely nothing to it... and I high-tailed it to the farmhouse kitchen. There Robert—the paralysing effect of shock having left him at the same moment as I did—immediately joined me, cowardly leaving his post and bucket.

The trouble with the younger generation, I told him, was they had no guts.

In the event he would have had a long time to wait. Rosie did her worst an hour later.

Poor Rosie. We didn't know it then but at the end of the month she would be dead.

She did not pick up from the calving but mooned about listlessly and refused her nuts—something I should never have believed possible. Suspecting incipient milk fever Gordon injected calcium but it made her no better. As yet there was very little growth on the fields but here and there in the garden I found long fresh grass and I cut it and fed it to her. She ate it quite eagerly at first but after a few days even this lost its appeal and lay wilting in her trough under Rhoda's covetous eyes. Rosie was constipated too—something else I found incredible. Hoping that exercise might do the trick I let them out into a field for a few hours. On the way back through the yard Rosie fell down.

I nearly dropped myself next morning when I opened the cowhouse door. Rosie was stretched out on her back, legs straight up in the air, and half strangled by the chain which was dragging her head backwards so tightly that its metal toggle fastener was jammed. I climbed over her inert body and tore frantically at the chain. It was immovably locked.

I thought of sawing it free and searched the workshop for a hacksaw. In my panic I couldn't think where Gordon kept them and even had I found one I knew I couldn't saw through all that metal before Easter.

On shaking legs I ran to the phone and dialled Will Arrowsmith's number. The number was engaged. I hurried back to the cowhouse followed by an alarmed Antony. Gordon had departed for work long since. Robert, too, had left for his school in Whitby but Antony, the middle one of our three sons, still attended the village school and his taxi wasn't due for a few more minutes.

Because he was usually the only one around Antony was closely acquainted with my reactions when faced with an emergency. Whenever danger or crisis threatens I am thoroughly dependable.

'Don't just follow me about,' I screamed. 'Keep on trying to ring Will.' I tussled again with the chain.

'What do you mean, it's still engaged?' I yelled when he reappeared a couple of minutes later. People had no business to be using their phones when I might be ringing on a matter of life and death.

Antony quaked and said he'd try again. I pushed past him and snatched the phone myself. But it defied even me.

'You'll have to go up there on your bike!'

Antony was disposed to quibble and prattle about taxis but I soon put a stop to that. He pedalled off up the one-in-four hill and I alternately wrung my hands in the cowhouse and tried to ring Will in the kitchen. I got through to Will's wife, Joan, just as Antony tumbled off his bike breathless and speechless in their farmyard.

Will and his man, George were running across our garage field as I staggered down the yard for the umpteenth time. Together we raced for the cowhouse and burst through the doorway at the very second Rosie rolled on to her knees and clambered unsteadily to her feet. In a spasm of heightened hysteria I nearly pushed her down again.

But Rosie was very ill, I knew. The vet diagnosed both milk fever and slow fever. I shall remember the acetate smell of the slow fever for the rest of my life. To make matters worse, she had badly cut a teat in her struggle to stand up.

A few days later she collapsed again—not frighteningly on her back this time but just as solidly immovable as before. And this time I was on the wrong side, helplessly stuck in her food trough.

Rosie had run off a lot of weight during her illness but from this angle it wasn't noticeable. Her stomach rose in front of me like Great Gable. I might have stridden over her had my legs been six feet long. I could have jumped with a few yards run up, but from a standing start, never. So there I was lifting first one foot then the other like a shire horse marking time to a slow march with Robert at the farther side looking as baffled as I was. Short of sprouting wings escape was hopeless.

Suddenly Robert perked up. 'Dad's home,' he shouted. 'I can hear the car. I'll go and get him.' He barged out of the door, turned and bobbed back.

'Wait there,' he said encouragingly.

The vet came to see Rosie again bringing drips and injections. We dosed her, too, with pints of thick black molasses and Will called every day with remedies of his own—he was almost as concerned as we were. But Rosie looked worse every day.

Will stood watching her intently one morning. 'That's not just slow fever. There's summat more than that. I've niver seen owt like it afore.'

He was right. Mr Cardew came again and told us that Rosie had adhesions in the bowel. With very little hope he suggested half a pound of Epsom salts in water for two days . . .

It didn't work and the next day Rosie left us. We were all very upset. Though she lacked the obvious personality of the other two cows, she was one of our Westwath originals and would always hold a special place in our hearts.

But life must go on, as they say, and at Westwath it was going on with a vengeance.

Bluebell calved and for the first time in her life did not go down with milk fever. We couldn't think why not. Bluebell going down with milk fever was an annual event like Guy Fawkes night and we felt positively insecure without it.

Nine months before, she had been served through the agency of the Milk Marketing Board by a beef shorthorn bull. The AI man was quite chuffed about it. 'We don't get so many asking for these old breeds nowadays. More's the pity.'

And if appearances were anything to go by it was, because that calf was the most beautiful we have ever had. Also it was our first home-produced heifer. Ten coal black Aberdeen Angus bulls in a row and now a pure white— apart from an enhancing fine, black outlining to her ears and sweeping black eye-lashes—bewitching girl, far too angelic for this world. Gordon was enchanted with her and called her his gorgeous girl friend. We named her Snowdrop—or Galanthus nivalis for short.

Life was still going on—Storky, one of our two ginger kittens, suddenly grew up and gave birth to a kitten of her own, and Gordon, being of the opinion that four cats already were quite enough, quickly removed it. To our relief Storky was quite unconcerned and indeed seemed unaware that she had had a kitten at all. I only mention it because later events proved how wrong we were.

Bluebell, as I said, didn't have milk fever. She opted for mastitis instead.

I knew it for cruddle the second I squeezed her teat and nobbly string came out. Cruddle is Will's word which we prefer to curd, though given the choice we would have neither.

The vet coming in passed the doctor going out but the vet was Mr Burn himself this time and, it being our regular doctor's weekend off, the doctor was a locum from another village. So they passed each other without recognition which, considering how many points go against us at this place, counted as a try in our favour at least.

4

Interior decorating

Mother had become thoroughly run down and, on the doctor's advice, had gone to stay with my cousin in York for a while. It would be a good opportunity, I thought, to decorate her bedroom.

Straight after milking, with the prospect of a good clear day in front of me, I spread dust-covers and newspapers, prized the lid off the paint tin, stirred the contents vigorously and was just cleaning off the stick with the paintbrush—glancing approvingly through the window as I did so, at the nicely growing grass in the hayfield—when my day was suddenly blighted.

Sheep, I saw—the bane of my life. Six of them, noses to the ground, progressing inexorably across the field like a plague of locusts.

The moment I laid hold of the window push-bar I was aware that I'd been over-enthusiastic with the paint stirring. My hands were lathered in the stuff and by the time I had flung open the casement and hurled out a few choice words it was all over the glass and in my hair as well.

That was typical. Every single time sheep and I cross swords they emerge victorious and I retire covered in confusion. And, on this occasion, paint as well.

Over the years, our confrontations have ranged from desultory skirmishes to full pitched battles, initially with our own flock, then, since its dispersal, with what seems like the entire ovine population of North Yorkshire which much prefers the grass of our little fields to anywhere else in the country. They have become accustomed to the sound of my voice and the interesting way it cracks in mid screech, so this crowd felt no immediate urge to stop what they were doing.

With a flash of precognition I knew this was going to be a day like a number of others I had endured. I ran downstairs and up the steps to the hayfield where, when they noticed my battlecry, two of the sheep raised their heads wearily. For a moment.

But I wasn't beaten. I brought up my heavy guns.

'Jess,' I yelled. 'Sheep!'

A black and white hearthrug flew up the steps and charged into the arena. It sat squarely in the middle of the field behind the fleeing flock and looked eagerly at me for instructions. Where did I want 'em? Up a tree or at the bottom of the beck?

New Zealand wouldn't have been far enough in my opinion but I told her to do the best she could. Jess's best was always very good and if it hadn't been for the subversive actions of humans she would have cleared up the matter within minutes, leaving me to return to the decorating. As it was, she chased them out of the fields and across the road. Where the stone hump-backed bridge crossed the beck the ewes jumped through a broken fence down to the grassy bank below. Jess followed, pursuing them up the steep crags of the Scar, dodging between hazels, rowans and ashes which clung to it by willpower, until she was satisfied that they were clear of Westwath property, when she returned to help me scowl disgustedly at the smashed fence.

This was our own fence, and it incorporated a stile because it was the point whence a footpath started. Many were the times—about once a month whenever we found the thing broken—we speculated on the manner of being who climbed over it. A rogue elephant was one suggestion.

Once we actually saw the creature in action.

That particular day I was standing up to my shins in water underneath the bridge closely involved with a well-armoured thorn bush as I attempted to thwart a maquis-like manoeuvre by a patrol of potential mutton. Binnie Brown, our neighbour, lending a helping hand, was repairing the stile.

Bent double and wielding a heavy hammer she fought to hold up a length of wood which seemed to have a will of its own. Every time she took a swipe at the nail the rail dropped to the ground and barked her knuckles. Hot and red-faced she straightened up and was astounded to learn that she was supporting twelve stone of solid man who, scorning sissyish expressions like please or excuse me, and too impatient to wait, had his size eleven walking boot squarely on the rail.

Well, that rail had gone again. Jess sat on guard and hoped the sheep would just try something, and I went home for hammer, nails and another length of wood.

When I had finished the repair and climbed over twice to make sure it was solid and Jess had leaped it the same number of times just to show that she could, we turned back to the road. There plumb in the middle of the bridge *behind me* stood the same six demonic sheep.

With a yell of disbelief and rage Jess and I gave chase. Around the corner and up the one in four hill we all pounded. The sheep's egress was explained. For yards and yards along the sinuously winding hill the fence was a wreck.

This fence was not ours. Who owned it no one knew. It was a flimsy barrier between the road and the other side of the Scar. It was variously thought by the locals to be the responsibility of the Duchy, the Forestry or either of two other large estates in the neighbourhood but was, in practice, sketchily maintained by farmers whose sheep strayed through it or whose land they strayed on to. Half a dozen farmers had patched it up at some time or other but, as we were the nearest, it was usually us and, in particular, me.

There were times when it seemed to me that the greater part of my life had been wasted on that fence. Not only had it absorbed my best years but pounds and pounds of expensive nails as well. The surviving original square-cut uprights had rotted away inside and, if not judged to a nicety, a nail knocked through the outer shell disappeared suddenly and could be heard rattling down the hollow shaft like a coin in a slot machine. Eventually I started tying the fence up with baler-band, the same as everyone else.

I should like, here and now, to nominate binder-twine— baler-band, billy-band, call it what you will—for a design award. Without it half the farms in the country would fall to pieces. And half the farmers, too. It is worn as belts around coats, and to hold up trousers. Tied around the bottoms of trouser-legs it keeps out snow, and it makes passable emergency boot-laces. Lots of it plaited into a rope then coiled and sewn to make a large disc made a super mat for the kitchen. This was done as a surprise for me by Antony and his friend Andy Arrowsmith, both of whom, long before it was completed, didn't half wish they had never started. Not to be outdone, Gordon and our friend Denis reseated a set of rush-bottomed chairs with it (rushes being unobtainable at the time) and they look better than they did originally. All this after being used for the purpose it was made... binding straw and hay bales.

For fencing it was invaluable. Square lashings, diagonal lashings, hitches and knots, that fence had them all, and by the time I had finished at lunchtime that day, it looked like an exercise in macramé.

We had a hurried meal of fish fingers, four-year-old Roger and I. Judging this to be no time for qualms I accepted his offer to wash up and hurried to the calf field with a bundle of hay for the calves' dinners. The morning had been an utter waste of time but with the stirks fed and watered and off my mind I should still have all the afternoon to work on mother's room.

As it turned out, it wasn't my mind they were off but the premises. The field was entirely devoid of cattle.

From where I stood by the securely fastened gate the whole long narrow pasture was in full view. Bounded on one side by an unbreached wall and on the other by the beck, stoppered at the far end by thick forest, it was a classic example of a locked room mystery, a cinch for Agatha Christie; another headache for me.

My heart almost slipped its moorings again but as I wrung my hands preparatory to going frantic I heard from the direction of the vegetable garden a sound that was beyond the capabilities of a Brussels sprout. It was Erik the Red, one of the calves, thoughtfully sniffing the rhubarb.

Muttering a short fervent prayer—in my imagination I could hear Mr Cardew flipping through his poison-book and stopping at oxalic acid—I drove Erik through the cabbages back to his field and shut him inside the hut. How he got into the vegetable garden without sprouting wings is a mystery to this day. His story that at one minute he was looking at a holly tree and thinking nice thoughts and the next, there he was in the rhubarb I am now, after much deliberation, inclined to accept.

There was no sign of the other four calves but, at least, there was a clue to the means of *their* decampment. Behind the hut in the least obvious place along the whole length of fence bordering the beck, a snapped-off post lay among trampled sheep netting. The beck enigmatically went about its business. Beyond it, also keeping its own counsel, Ghyll House farm's rough-grazing land, pot-holed and scrub-covered heaved its way into the distance.

Ignoring Erik, who with chin resting on the half door of the hut was offering to help in the search . . . *he* hadn't gone off like that, had he? . . . I crossed the beck by the footbridge and climbed to a vantage point. Silhouetted on the distant horizon a group of animals grazed peacefully. Seven of them, I saw as I toiled nearer, belonged to the Stewarts. The other four were ours.

As I panted over the last ridge Jasper lifted his head and looked at me as if he had never seen me before and returned contemptuously to his grazing. The rest preferred not to notice me at all. Only the Stewarts' beasts looked at me for any length of time—with the affronted stare of polite company troubled by a gate-crasher.

They looked on superciliously as I thumped those bottoms that belonged to me. The bottoms moved slightly forward, not as a result of my goading but because the grass was a little fresher further along. We continued like this for some time, the calves shuffling slowly in circles with me stumbling on their heels, round and round in the little scrub-girded amphitheatre like a small-time repertory company attempting an ambitious production of *Riders of the Purple Sage*. We were just passing for the umpteenth time the remains of a long-deceased sheep I should have preferred not to have seen even once, when the cast was suddenly reinforced by extras who boosted the show no end. It was Matt and Joe Stewart with an escort of dogs.

I must mention here that the reason my own dog was not under-foot was that Jess was, as she never let us forget, a *sheep*-dog and not a *cow*-dog. Show her a calf and she was off like a rocket in the opposite direction. It was weak of her, she knew, but there it was . . . anything under a year old and she came over all funny.

Jasper, the eldest of our beasts, was still inclined to argue. A noted free-thinker since the moment, two minutes after he was born eleven months earlier, when with lowered head he had threatened to see me off the farm and only two hours after that had broken out of his pen, flattened a hurdle and found his mother across the yard, he had never given us cause to doubt it.

But in Matt's dogs he had met his match.

Once their leader was seen to be in retreat the other animals gave no more trouble but allowed themselves to be trotted in a bunch down to the beck and projected into and across it. The efforts of their new friends to follow were thwarted by the dogs who drove them over the hill and out of the story.

Even then I could not return to my decorating because

there was the gap in the fence to repair. More binder twine and some good stout non-yew branches took care of that, and with the escape route safely blocked I unbolted the calf-hut door to let Erik the Red out. It was unnecessary. He wasn't there.

Well all right, I had left the top section open but how was I to know he could leap five feet over the lower door and slot himself through a hole not much more than two feet wide. It simply wasn't possible. I found him back in the rhubarb, apparently spirited there by some mysterious power.

For a little while after that I sat on the settee with my feet up. Not—to keep the record straight—because I was womanishly feeling the strain but because Roger, having finished washing the pots and the sink and the floor, had set out in search of me and taken a nasty tumble that could be cured only by a cuddle and a chapter of *Winnie the Pooh*. After which it was time to give a thought to Gordon's evening meal which would have to be something other than fish fingers.

It was not, Gordon always said, that he didn't *like* fish fingers even though they were made from specially grown artificial fish. But he *preferred* something else—like dry bread and water. So I put meat in the oven, prepared vegetables and was just dashing around to the compost heap with the peelings when once more I was alerted to Action Stations. The garage field and main road were infested with a plague of Friesian cattle.

This might have meant that the events of the day had sent me over the edge into fantasy. But no. When I battled my way through the crowd of very solid bodies in the field and against the black and white tide surging up the road, it was to find that someone had left open the gate into Charlie Rawden's wood where his herd had been grazing.

By the time that episode was concluded, milking done, the evening meal eaten and Roger put to bed I was willing to concede that I had done enough decorating for one day.

Painting, I complained, as I tugged a comb through my white-highlighted, glued-together hair, had tired me out.

5

Rhoda does her bit

Shortly after that I discovered the identity of the owners of the land at the far side of the ravine, ergo, the owners of that controversial fence. I happened to be passing the time of day with two members of the Forestry Commission who were inspecting their property where its downhill rush is abruptly halted by the fence which divides it from our fields, and they casually dropped into the conversation an item of news that rocked me to my very foundations.

The Forestry Commission, they told me, were considering making that sliver of land on the top of the Scar into a picnic spot by removing the fence altogether.

My sensations can only be compared with those of folk living on Dartmoor were they to learn that from now on Princetown Prison would operate without walls or bars.

I couldn't sleep that night. I spent it counting sheep. Sheep running down the Scar, sheep rock-hopping across the beck, sheep swarming over the new picnic site and descending the hill in droves. Sheep like a white-capped river flooding into our little fields and engulfing the lot of us.

I went downstairs at 5 a.m. and typed a petition.

The evening of that day was all apple-green, gold and skylark-speckled but my mind wasn't on it as, accompanied by Roger, I marched militantly over the moor to Ghyll House Farm where I found Matt and Joe in the big barn surrounded by sheep. An awful lot of sheep.

'That fence,' said Joe when I poured out my story, 'is a rum do.' Rum is the strongest adjective I have ever heard Joe use. 'Niver could find out who it belonged to and we've patched it up oorselves, like, time and time agin. Why if they tek that away there'll be nowt to stop sheep at all. Aye, we'll be glad to sign petition.'

Really, I thought later that evening when, with the boys put to bed, Gordon and I drove up to Castle Farm, this was turning into quite a social occasion. Normally weeks went by during which the closest contact we had with neighbours was spotting an unidentifiable figure guiding a tractor over some distant hill. Which was why, some time later and with Will Arrowsmith's willingly given signature lined up under the Stewarts', we stood chatting for an hour in a cutting wind up at Ellers Farm.

For all that Ellers Farm was distant from Westwath only a matter of half a mile as the crow flies, a steep forest lay between them, and the way round by road was three times greater. Moreover, it was a road leading only to Ellers and Rowan Head Farms so was not one which we often travelled. Usually we saw Mrs Rawdon only when she delivered—or we collected—our Christmas goose, so getting together twice in one year was really living it up.

I believe she was pleased to see us too. We with our petition were an entertaining change from the hens and geese of which her world was chiefly composed. Small, apple-cheeked and resilient, she was, we happened to know, suffering from a cracked rib, yet for the whole of that hour she held in one hand a large galvanized bucket full to the top with eggs. It didn't seem to cross her mind to put it down.

Next day I collected more names for the petition. All the signatures bore a marked resemblance to one another—spidery and wavering owing to the unstable nature of various things the paper was rested on. The top rail of a gate was the choice of one farmer, an oil drum another, a bale of straw (a perforated signature that one), and the more level surfaces of sundry farm implements. I was quite sorry when there was no one else to visit.

The petition, I am happy to record, was successful; and some time later (partly thanks to the involvement of the NFU and the Highways people who pointed out that gappy fencing there rendered the cattle-grid up the road useless) the Forestry Commission renewed the fence altogether.

And with my mind disencumbered of that I turned to happier things.

We were joyfully looking forward to the weekend. It would be the Whitsuntide holiday and our friends, Kath and Denis Ward, with their children Janet and David, were coming to stay with us for the week. Hitherto they had been able to visit us only for a fortnight each August and there was always a superabundance of news to catch up on. News of a full year's happenings at Westwath read like a decade of anyone else's. Like an old Norse saga really, but more action-packed and gory. A fortnight was not long enough to relate it all.

We were dying to see them again and to introduce them to the beauty of Westwath in springtime. And if that doesn't illustrate the softening effect of time I don't know what does, because never yet had the Wards set foot on the place without confusion, chaos and disaster following. Flood, fire and pestilence—we have had them all. Although they were *there* it was nothing that they *did* and we do not blame them for it. All the same it's funny...

Although I did not know it as I went happily about my preparations, the stage was already being set for the next drama.

I ought to have realized that something was in the wind when Rhoda calved a fortnight before she was due. Down in the inevitable inconvenient place—the marshy end of the back field.

Unlike Bluebell and Rosie, Rhoda knew her Dr Spock so I had no fears for the new baby's welfare. Even so, I watched from a distance the calf's sudden unappreciative introduction to the buttercups. Rhoda's motherliness was not of the 'There, there, little one' school. The comforting properties of *Winnie the Pooh* she scorned to consider. With a tongue like a nutmeg-grater she raked the infant into the ground and soothed him with a murmur reminiscent of the Humber lightship in a fog. Like, possibly, the same lightship in a changing tide, she swung round and knocked him over each time his search for nourishment took him to the wrong end. Her brisk no-nonsense method worked very well and in no time at all he was washed, made presentable and was tucking in to his first meal.

I was delighted. Good old Rhoda—what a wonderful mother she was. So wonderful that when at milking time I went to fetch them all in she lowered her head in an unfriendly manner, said she wasn't coming in and if I laid so much as a finger on her son she would have something to say about that as well.

And Bluebell, *Bluebell* whose interest in calves was slightly less than her enthusiasm for the financial index, supported her. Touch one hair of that babe, she said, looking up from under her eyebrows, and she would have me.

It was not that I was intimidated but the time I was wasting while the four of us did a sort of barn dance in the rushes was annoying so I went home and called out the family.

We felt like the Sheriff and Deputies of Deadman's Gulch, Robert, Antony, Jess and I, as we advanced in line towards the jaw-grinding outlaws. Level gaze met level gaze—it was a scene fraught with suspense. Had it come to a shoot-out I reckon it would have been touch and go...

It was the wheelbarrow that won the day. (We always brought home new calves in the wheelbarrow because it was one of the many obscure instructions our predecessor at the farm had given us. We learned eventually that, given a little encouragement, the animal would walk in under its own steam.) The barrow distracted Rhoda for a moment.

While she gave it a thorough hoovering with her wide wet nose I slipped around her, scooped up the calf behind the knees and, as Rhoda pivoted a fraction too late, dumped him in the straw-lined conveyance.

Then it was a race for home across the lumpy field, the wheelbarrow and my internal organs jolting and yawing at each tussock. Robert, at a crouching lope, held down the calf. Antony and Jess alternately drove on and fended off the excitable mother and her crony.

As the other calfpens were already occupied by a pop-eyed audience, we had made up quarters for the new boy in the annexe to the cowhouse which had its own doorway into the yard. Antony ran ahead and opened the door while Robert and I in the final stages of exhaustion and with a badly shifting cargo staggered over the last few yards of uneven paving to the safe haven. But ill-fortune overtook us. Right in the very doorway the cargo unexpectedly, considerably and disastrously increased. Rhoda, realizing that her son was about to disappear from her sight, let heart over-rule her head and climbed into the barrow to keep him company.

Already overloaded well past plimsoll line, the barrow capsized and sank with all hands, and with Robert, Antony, Rhoda, the calf, the barrow and myself filling the doorway to capacity, things looked very nasty indeed.

I suppose it was all over in a few moments, but it seemed like a lifetime. We emerged with only one casualty—a handle snapped off the wheelbarrow. True, Rhoda was now inside the pen with the calf instead of lined up with Bluebell in the cowhouse but we can't have everything. Thanks to a bucket of warm bran mash held out as a carrot we got her out eventually and bedded her down in the cowhouse for the night. And that, I thought with satisfaction, was our entire herd calven for the year.

The stage was now set, the orchestra tuning up in the pit and, at five o'clock the next morning, the curtain was about to rise.

It was the fifth morning in a row that I had wakened at

that time and I was fed up about it. Always a poor sleeper, I had been averaging only four or five hours a night for weeks (I do hope no one is going to suggest that I needed to take more exercise . . .) and my brain was so sluggish that I was hardly responsible for my actions.

The night before, for instance . . . You remember those illustrations in the old-time *Boys' Own Paper* and the like? That one where Caruthers, the young, clean-cut sub-lieutenant had pulled back the bed sheet and drawn away in horror, one hand raised to ward off the surprised and resentful, rearing cobra? Well, when dropping with exhaustion I had pulled back *my* sheet, I looked exactly like that. Only it wasn't a snake I was gawping at but a loaf of bread.

What I had done with the hot water bottle I don't know but, no, it wasn't in the breadbin.

Anyway there I was, awake again. Gordon absolutely refused to be—even though I flounced about with all the feeling I could muster—so I went downstairs and luxuriated in a welter of self-pity.

'I'm so *tired*,' I moaned aloud to the empty kitchen. 'The Wards are coming today and there's the baking to finish. And I suppose,' I howled—though not too loudly because I didn't want Gordon coming down and spoiling it—'I shall have to milk the *cows* as well!'

I made some dreadful buns and a rather nice trifle then, hurriedly because time was getting on and I could hear Gordon moving about upstairs, gathered up the milking buckets and set off down the garden path passing, en route, the cats homing in for breakfast from four different directions.

It was a beautiful May morning but I cut it dead. Still reciting my grievances (the *cats* to feed, *Jess* to feed, *calves* to feed, *cows* etc.) I shovelled dairy-nuts into buckets and opened the lower half-door of the cowhouse. Rhoda was stretched senseless on the floor her mouth flecked with foam and her body enveloped in steam.

My jaw dropped. Not *Rhoda*. Rhoda *never* had milk fever. I hadn't even considered the possibility.

I forgot all about my role as one of the world's oppressed and ran for Gordon who was in the kitchen wondering what on earth had happened to the milking buckets.

As he, assisted by Robert, set up the subcutaneous calcium drip I dialled the vet's well-known number. Rhoda looked very ill and we were taking no chances.

It was ages before the surgery answered. I was beginning to think the vet was expecting our call and had left town. It transpired he *had* left town. His holidays had started in the nick of time and his place had been taken that very day by a locum, Mr Williams. Mr Williams was very handsome and as he injected into Rhoda's vein I stood close by helpfully in my jeans and boots and hoped I looked like Doris Day in *Calamity Jane*.

I was almost pleased when, later that evening, we had to call him out again. Rhoda, though now conscious, had made no effort to stand. For the umpteenth time we watched air bubbles dance in the calcium bottle. Calcium at Westwath seemed to flow like fizzy pop. We should have felt much better had we known that this was to be the last case of milk fever for some years.

If she was not on her feet in the morning, said Mr Williams, I was to be sure to ring him again.

Oh, I *would*, I assured him earnestly, treating him to my dazzling Doris Day smile.

I did too, but before that another of our crazy comedies had played itself out.

6

Nocturnal adventures

Missing the vet by a cat's whisker on his first visit that day, the Wards arrived for their holiday. The sight of them did me the world of good and I completely forgot I was tired. After their two, Janet and David, and our own three children were tucked up for the night, we talked long and late, reminiscing about previous years' adventures and, distance lending enchantment, laughing our heads off over them.

'Remember last year,' said Denis, 'when all three cows came in season together and Bluebell went berserk?'

'And, the same day, Roger lost use of his legs and we thought it was polio?' said Kath.

'And Mr Stewart's beasts got into the garden and ran all over it,' contributed Janet. 'And Bluebell thought they were bulls and tried to jump over the fence and...'

'Stupid animal,' said Gordon. 'Couldn't tell stirk from butter.'

'Now Rhoda's poorly,' said Kath sympathetically. 'I wonder,' she went on before anyone could gag her, 'what else will happen this year?'

We were soon to find out. At one forty-five in the morning, to be precise. On the one night, in desperation, I had taken a sleeping pill.

It was Kath who roused me. She didn't want to, she

assured me when she had my ear if not my complete and eager attention, but the phone wouldn't stop ringing no matter how hard she ignored it.

Now that she mentioned it I recognized the sound. I had thought it was the dawn chorus again.

Kath seemed to expect that I should do something about it though I couldn't think what. The floor was unsteady and the stairs, as we descended them, at an unusual angle. It might have been better had I remembered to pick up the torch from the bedside table but such advanced thinking was far beyond my mogadon-impregnated mind, and we crunched blindly on bare feet through the Lego bricks scattered widespread and thickly over the dining-room floor. We groped through the inner hall with its as yet uncarpeted concrete floor into the darkened living-room and the source of all the row.

Unsteadily I picked up the receiver and the noise stopped. Just in time I refrained from replacing it. There was a woman's voice nattering from the earpiece. It was not making any sense.

It kept repeating that it was *Binnie*. Well all right, Binnie lived in the next house up the hill but she was a non-farming neighbour so why was she going on about pigs and Land-Rovers and tractors? At a quarter to two in the morning? I thought she was crackers.

Apparently the feeling was mutual.

'Listen, Joyce,' the voice enunciated in carefully controlled tones, 'there is a Land-Rover stuck on the hill. It can't get up. Will Gordon come with the tractor..?'

'Gordon's in bed,' I said owlishly, 'and *our* tractor's not big enough... *Who* did you say it was?'

There was a sigh from the other end of the line. 'Never mind. Steven's on his way down to you.'

'Our tractor...' I began, but the line had gone dead.

There was a rap on the back door. Kath opened it.

'... isn't strong enough,' I said to Steven standing in the doorway.

Somewhere between the bedroom and the telephone

44

table I had acquired a box of matches. I struck one or two to peer into the newcomer's face. Politely Steven removed the box from my unresisting hand and lighted the gas lamp.

No doubt Kath understood the ensuing conversation better than I did. It still seemed coloured with pigs and Land-Rovers. We trudged painfully back through the Lego and woke Gordon who, naturally, had slept through everything. *He* got hung up on the pigs, too, and he hadn't had a sleeping pill.

Dazedly he got out of bed and I rolled into his warm place.

A couple of minutes later—or so it seemed to me—he flopped back in again. The bounce woke me slightly.

'Aren't you going?' I asked sleepily.

He groaned like one who has known suffering. 'We've been. It's half past three, and I think I've just lost us a very good neighbour.'

'Who? Binnie?' I remembered that shrilling telephone, 'Good!'

'Not Binnie. Will.' His tones were regretful.

'Uh, Will? Not *Will*,' I was startled into wakefulness. 'What's Will got to do with it..?'

Gordon flapped a weary hand. 'Oh, go to sleep. Tell you in the morning.' He sighed and went out like a light.

It was very late in the morning with the arrival of a bleary-eyed Binnie before the whole story came together and made sense.

She and Steven had just gone to bed and turned off the generator, Binnie recounted, flopping into a chair and shakily lighting a cigarette, when there was this knock at the door. Half past one in the morning and a knock at the door. She shook her head disbelievingly.

Steven had taken a torch and gone downstairs and there was this white-faced hysterical woman pleading for help on the doorstep. The woman was weeping and wringing her hands, said Binnie. It was just like a Victorian melodrama—all that was missing was the baby. Next minute there was a wail and the woman ran back to the gate and picked one up out of the nettles. A baby! A *baby*! Would we believe it!

Oh-ohh, they were convinced by then, said Binnie, that it was a confidence trick of some sort. But there was the baby covered in nettle-rash, poor thing, so what could they do?

Anyway, between sobs, the woman told them that she and her family had come all the way from the West Riding—they'd been on the road all day. They were moving into a farm cottage way up the dale but the Land-Rover had broken down on the hill. The baby was hungry and they didn't know *what* to do...

Binnie drew them indoors while Steven went out to investigate. The Land-Rover was real enough. So was the trailer that was slewed into the bank at the bottom of the hill. It was a big trailer of the horsebox type and was packed to overflowing with what looked like household goods. In the Land-Rover were several more children and a young man who was almost as distraught as his wife.

The clutch had gone, he said, on the hill. They'd come down backwards—he thought they were going to turn over... Could Steven possibly given them a tow?

Steven took a closer look at the trailer. As well as assorted furniture it contained an awful lot of what appeared to be fat sacks of cattle-food.

No way would his car tow that, said Steven. However, he might just be able to pull the Land-Rover—packed with mattresses though it was. What about uncoupling the trailer and parking it alongside the house until morning?

The young man blenched and looked wilder than ever. He couldn't do that, he said, because of the pigs.

Incredible though it seemed, there were two good pigs somewhere inside the trailer. Though Steven had been nearly right about the cattle-food—half a ton of pig meal, qualified its owner. He stood in a posture of defence as if he thought Steven was going to wrest the trailer from him by force, and refused point blank to part with it.

It was then that Binnie took the other children indoors—

the young man, passionately protecting his pigs, hardly noticed them go. These children, Binnie abstractedly saw, were in some inexplicable way also showing signs of advanced nettle rash as well as suffering from very nasty coughs. Compassionately she stirred up the fire and settled them cosily before it. Then she telephoned us.

The tractor, I would remember, said Gordon taking up the tale, had been last used and left by the vegetable patch, so he had had to drive it round the house and through the garden in the dark. Denis had been somewhere about, but couldn't see any better than Gordon could. He hoped he hadn't damaged anything. *I* hoped he hadn't damaged anything, I seconded.

(So that's what the row was, said Frankie and Tom, friends of ours who were staying in the bungalow for the week and had been drawn in to hear the story. It had wakened them up, they said. They had thought it was army tank manoeuvres on the moor and were drafting a letter of complaint about it. Honestly, I don't know how we keep *any* friends.)

When he saw the trailer, said Gordon, he knew straight away it was too much for our little Ferguson tractor. Why not, he suggested brightly, leave the trailer in our field for the night?

The young fellow explained fully and at length. Steven gave Gordon a feeling look.

So Gordon, being the sort who would never admit to being stuck even though a quicksand had closed a yard over his head, attached a chain to both vehicles and had a go.

Our hill is sign-posted as a one-in-four. That is an optimistic estimate. Parts of it are steeper. At each one of these sticky bits Gordon paused while Denis and Steven wedged rocks behind the trailer's wheels. Denis, who, after all, had been rudely awakened from early deep sleep—and this Binnie should have allowed for—didn't think to pick up a fresh stone at each stopping place but staggered uphill hugging his chosen rock to his waistline. This convulsed Binnie and her daughter, Judith, who, having left the young woman and her children to recover with hot drinks, had come out to watch the proceedings.

They laughed so much that they leaned for support on the roof of a little blue van which was parked off the road by the Forestry fence where the picnic site had been proposed. The van shook with their laughter.

They had lolled there helplessly for a full minute before it dawned on them why the van was there. Lying inside, apparently dumb and petrified with fear, were people who must have expected a quiet night's sleep.

It was the very tip of the hill which defeated the Fergie. The road there has been sliced off in an attempt to tame it but it still rears like the crest of a wave. The tractor reared as well. Gordon said that the front wheels actually left the ground but just as he thought it was all up with him the chain snapped, the Land-Rover and trailer backed hurriedly downhill and settled cosily into their original position tail-first up the bank.

And that was how Will came to be involved.

'You are a bloody nuisance but I'll come,' Will shouted when Gordon's handful of gravel rattled on the bedroom window. He hadn't said that straight away; there had been preliminaries—confusion brought about by the mention of pigs. Will's particular sleep-shattered unco-ordination tended to get snagged on the notion that the pigs were stolen and he wanted nothing to do with them.

Though why, Gordon said woundedly, Will should think that he, Gordon, would be mixed up with pinched pigs, he didn't know...

Will's bigger, stronger and newer tractor dragged the burden up the hill and along the road as far as the gate of Castle Farm. Wasn't Will going to tow him all the way to the cottage? the young man asked in alarm. Will hesitated.

'I—I'll give you a fiver!'

Will said he didn't want the fiver. It wasn't that. It was the fact that it was a good six miles farther and all those bloody gert hills... but he'd tell him what—leave trailer in t' yard owernight. He reckoned he could just about manage Land-Rover...

Gordon, Denis and Steven yawned. The result was a foregone conclusion. Will towed home the lot.

At half past three in the morning Binnie drove the young woman down the endless track that led only to the farm cottage. The young woman hopped out and ran over to the trailer and peered anxiously inside.

'Is the electric washer all right?' she asked.

'Honestly,' said Binnie, 'that trailer was like a conjurer's box. You wondered what else was in it.'

Assured that the washing machine was unharmed the woman returned and took the baby from Judith's arms. The rash, Binnie noticed, was worse than ever and the child seemed to have an awful head cold.

'Wrap them up and pop them into bed,' she instructed kindly, backing the car out of a muddy rut and turning for home.

'I can't thank you enough,' the woman called after them. She stood outside the cottage in the dead-end lane and shouted eagerly, 'Do call, won't you. Any time you're passing.'

There is a sequel to that story. Some days later Binnie phoned me. 'Judith is awfully poorly,' she said. 'She's got measles.'

7

Of birds and beasts

That was one way to get together with one's neighbours. A better one occurred a couple of evenings later when Kath accompanied me to a meeting of the parish Young Wives group. It was held that time in the beautiful sitting-room of a lovely old farmhouse whose owner entertained us with a filmshow of slides taken from sepia photographs of village scenes and worthies of long ago. Many featured the village street with a surprisingly large number of people—probably the entire population drawn out by the excitement—steadfastly facing the camera from random positions all over the traffic deserted road.

There were other pictures—buxom ladies in dark ground-length skirts of an amplitude that spoke of the wearers' no-nonsense attitude to undies, and defiant-looking men, all billy-cock hats and watch-chains, grouped around the doorway of the old Railway Hotel. The dog-cart which presumably had deposited them there was in the charge of a knickerbockered urchin who ought to have been in school. Those who *were* in school had also been recorded for posterity—a double row of large eyes and pinafores. Some of them, identified by our host, were claimed with varying degrees of hilarity as forebears by several of the Young Wives.

There was even—and I was tickled pink to recognize

it—a photo of our own house taken at the turn of the century, the incumbents of the time standing proudly in front of it clutching to their bosoms a couple of bee-skeps. I bet they are the very same coiled straw skeps that lie in the hayloft to this day. And, golly, look at the house walls all smothered in creeper. All that remains of that are the hand-forged nails it was tied to. Our amazement grows—those small domes of greenery peeping over the orchard wall... they can't be..? They *are*! The yew and monkey-puzzle trees that now look down on us from their towering heights.

How quaint the pictures were. The old lady with her pail and three-legged stool, for instance, milking her cow in the middle of a field. We all laughed like drains at that one. Who, in this hygienic, mechanized age, would go about their dairying like that?

Well me, as a matter of fact. The very next day.

You will remember leaving Rhoda recumbent in the cowhouse and me batting my eyelashes at the vet way back on page 42. Well, next morning—after an interval while we and our neighbours larked around with pigs and measles—the scene and characters were pretty much the same. Except that in my case, I felt less like Doris Day and more like the original Calamity Jane who must have been well over a hundred by then. Rhoda, though looking brighter and dealing with food with the thoroughness of a dustcart pulverizer, had shown no inclination to get on to her feet.

Mr Williams arrived with a Bagshaw hoist. This is a simple but efficient arrangement of chains and pulleys plus a clamp which fits under the cow's pelvis. The chain, passed over a convenient roof beam and run through the pulleys, firmly and steadily lifted the cow's hindquarters. We had not seen this apparatus before and were most impressed. So was Rhoda—her eyes bulged with surprise as her rear-end ascended heavenwards. Hurriedly she arranged her front legs to match, Mr Williams slightly lowered the hoist and Rhoda made a three-and-a-half-point landing. Her right hind foot, we were dismayed to see, was knuckled under.

Frantically working the teats like pistons, I milked her before she could collapse again. Then Gordon took over and massaged the bent ankle joint.

Rhoda stood with a long-suffering expression on her face, snorting gently now and then to let us know what a waste of time it all was because she wasn't going to be better for *ages*. Probably a week. In fact she was going to lie down now and if we could just bring her a few nuts and the odd bale of hay... Hurriedly Gordon slipped the chain and turned her towards the door. She moved out to the field, limping dramatically like a particularly unlucky refugee from Culloden and, in the evening, limped back in again to subside in a heap on the floor like one who hadn't made it. Luckily Mr Williams had left the hoist with us. We used it then, and again the following morning.

I awaited the next milking time apprehensively because the vet had called in a hurry and taken the hoist to another case. Comforting though it was to learn we were not the only ones with problems, nevertheless I couldn't quite see myself oops-a-daisying Rhoda with biceps alone. Then Gordon had an idea. He had been watching Rhoda carefully over these last few days, he said, and had noticed that although she was unable to get to her feet on the unyielding concrete floor of the cowhouse, outside, by digging her hooves into the soft turf and rolling resolutely, she could do it—just.

There was nothing else for it, he said in the manner of one who had made the decision at great personal sacrifice, I should have to milk her where she stood. Right there in the middle of the field.

So there I was—while the rest of England's farmers fitted teat-cups and set machines chunking in their immaculate milking parlours—shuffling with my stool and cockly bucket over tussocks and cowpats after a restless cow, with respect for the old lady in the photograph mounting with each drop of shed sweat.

I only hoped, I said fervently, no Young Wives happened to drop by. On the credit side, it wasn't raining.

Fortunately it stayed dry because alfresco milking continued all week. There was some improvement in my lot because we had progressed to a tethering rope on the corner support to the hayshed and, with someone leaning heavily against Rhoda's stern to prevent her swinging at anchor, it was possible to milk from a stationary position.

Then came the morning when Rhoda, announcing she'd had enough of all that messing about, walked firmly into the cowhouse. From then on, apart from a tendency to limp whenever she felt like stirring something up, Rhoda was her old self.

All these things are sent to try us, which is probably the reason we were visited with the blue tit plague. Not that we should look upon blue tits as a plague under normal circumstances. All birds are welcome here—with the possible exception of jays, who strip the winter food-table and attack their smaller brethren. To us birds are one of life's pleasures and here at Westwath there is a wide variety to enjoy.

As I sit here at my window this winter morning I can see several blue, coal, and great tits, the latter tapping away like woodpeckers in their quest for insects. On the same errand a tree-creeper spirals up the cherry tree—there are usually one or two of those about; on the outer branches a pair of chaffinches dance. On his accustomed perch, the fourth pale from the right on the garden gate, sits a robin. Another clings sideways to a stiff, dead phlox stalk. Robins, we know, jealously guard their own territory but several boundaries must meet in our garden because it is commonplace for half a dozen or more to be seen there at one time. Yesterday one sat on my boot as I scattered crumbs. On the path a blackbird is attacking a fallen apple.

Simply to list bird visitors to Westwath would be a tedious waste of time—I might just as well refer you to *Thorburn's Birds* and have done with it, but there are some special pleasures.

The woodpeckers, green and pied, who laugh at us from the trees across the beck, wagtails and dippers curtsying to their reflections from water-girt rocks to a musical accompaniment from warblers of many sorts. There was the time a flock of tiny birds, dozens strong, ganged up on a marauding kestrel. Entirely surrounded by the agitated, scolding cloud the larger bird moved off, lazily circling and planing to a great height and distance. It was a complete rout.

There is the cock pheasant who, with his numerous wives, struts about our fields knowing he is safe from the gun—though when he scratches out my newly-sowed peas each year I have serious doubts about him. We are amazed at pheasants' sensitivity to low rumbling noises. Any such sound, no matter how faint, always brings a response of an alarmed, 'Kok-kok-kok'. The rumble of thunder or, perhaps, distant quarry-blasting may be too faint for human ears to catch. We know it has taken place because our sash-window, an infallible seismograph, vibrates a warning. We stop whatever we are doing and listen. Without fail from field or forest explode the answering metallic notes.

Two or three times a year I am galvanized by the arrival of the long-tailed tits. Suddenly becoming conscious of a soft but busy whistling I yell to my startled family, 'Hurry, hurry! They're coming. Be quick or you'll miss them!' We all fall over each other as we rush outside. Usually the boys go back in again when they discover the excitement is only about birds but I stand and watch with pleasure. In they come, perhaps a dozen of them in a string, flying in undulating swoops from tree to tree, their elegant tails so much longer than their bodies, their colouring a delicate pink and white with black. Last year they brought their babies and even Roger was impressed by those.

From all that, you will appreciate that we are not unmoved by the charm of birds and will understand that Gordon had been tried beyond human endurance when he proclaimed in a voice strangled with emotion that if he could catch the little beggars he'd wring their necks!

They had eaten the putty out of the window frames that had been newly put in the previous autumn. Not only that but they had done it *three times*.

The first occasion was immediately after the builders left us. Gordon replaced the putty himself muttering darkly that he had just *paid* to have this done and was wasting time and money doing it again. He painted it over with undercoat. He would have applied a top coat, too, had the birds left it alone long enough.

He puttied the frames for the third time, alternately worrying about whether the paint would poison the birds and saying what he would do to them if it didn't and they ate the stuff again.

This time to make *certain* they *couldn't* do it again he cut brown paper into narrow strips and painstakingly taped it over each length of new putty. Very odd, it looked. Though not nearly so odd as it did that Whitsuntide as Binnie and I leaned against the wall casually chatting in the sunshine. At least I was chatting. Binnie had ceased to listen and was staring transfixed at something beyond my shoulder.

Following the line of her pop-eyed gaze I saw the brown paper that outlined the windows—moving! *Heaving* like the tarpaulin sheet in an obstacle race. Those blasted blue tits were burrowing underneath it and, safe from all eyes, had eaten almost the last smear of putty.

Fortunately that week the weather continued fine and very warm because the stirks took off across the beck again. Not from behind the hut this time but through the fence, way down in the farthest corner by the parish boundary stone. In that place large rocks protrude from the water; owing to dry weather the beck was low anyway, so Denis, the children and I crossed by the same route.

We rounded up the runaways—not too difficult for six of us—and drove them back to the crossing place. They refused to enter the water . . . not *there*. They fancied that bit downstream where Matt and Joe had taken them last time. The part behind the calf-hut where Gordon had made a good repair with brand new sheep-netting.

At first we didn't think that was a very good idea and tried to persuade them to change their minds, but after losing them and regathering them twice, seemingly set to do so ad infinitum, we came round to their way of thinking.

Denis waded across, snipped through the wire fence and peeled it back. The rest of us hooshed the animals into the water and followed closely on their heels to discourage any afterthoughts. The beck here was deeper than at our original fording-place but once our boots had filled and we had all had a good shriek the iciness was much more bearable. Water streamed off animals and humans alike as we clambered up the farther bank on to home ground.

In other ways we differed. The first instinctive thought of the humans was relief at having won. The immediate reaction of the stirks was brighter. They high-tailed it down the field to the broken fence by the boundary stone with every intention of setting forth again.

They would have succeeded if it hadn't been for Erik the Red. Erik was so intoxicated with all this adventuring—just like his namesake, he'd been—that he felt called upon to lead this new foray. But a sudden flaring up of his old trouble—complete lack of sense of direction—caused him to overshoot the gap in the fence and heave to with his nose touching the date (1801) inscribed on the boundary stone. The others followed him but before they had time to reorientate were, themselves, overtaken by us in our waterlogged wellies.

We repaired that fence and Denis temporarily filled the break behind the calf-hut with a little-used gate especially taken off its hinges for the purpose.

And good gracious me! Now that I come to think of it, that's where it still is, eleven years on. We have been wondering where it had got to.

8

Bring hither the dratted calf

At the weekend the Wards departed still miraculously sound in wind and limb. About their minds I had reservations because they still intended to return for the usual fortnight in the summer. With this to look forward to we waved after their bus more cheerfully than usual and returned home to normality and another rodeo. One of Joe's heifers was paying a return visit in the hope of acquiring a mate. Erik, whose unexpected success as a Viking raider had given him precocious ideas, was doing his best to oblige but was hampered by lack of height and a particular operation performed on him by Gordon some months previously.

Fortunately, among the milling bodies was one we recognized as Joe's. With an action-packed John Wayne-type tactic, he was just encircling the heifer's neck with a noose. The boys and I chased off our stirks and returned to savour an interesting and unusual aspect of herdsmanship.

The heifer, in the lead, was just entering the beck, Joe, still attached to the other end of the halter, entered it a split second later, Gordon, hanging grimly on to the heifer's tail and almost sitting on his own heels, went in last. As a sea-anchor he wasn't much good. Both men were six-footers and hefty with it but they cut through the water like sharks and went straight up the steep bank opposite with complete disregard for the footpath, mowing down saplings and brushwood like nobody's business. Joe could congratulate himself on having a good beast there, I fancied.

The Wards, sitting innocently in their bus, must have been miles away from Westwath by then but we still blamed them for it. We agreed that it was because they were safely back in Hull that, on the following day our next big cattle round-up went so smoothly.

We had by then been living at Westwath for four years and the more perceptive of you will have realized that our farming methods were not as up to date as was desirable. I suppose they came somewhere this side of the elk's shoulder-blade plough but stopped short around about the decline of the horse. This situation was to change almost noticeably with the acquisition of modern equipment. Modern by our standards, that is.

The first thing we bought was an electric fence. We used it to divide the extremely steep lower part of the Scar field from the scarcely less extremely steep upper half. On this top part it was just possible to manoeuvre a tractor, so there we scattered fertilizer and raised a haycrop. When the grass grew again we would let in the cows to graze by which time, in pre-electric fence days, the growth on the lower part was long and coarse and the cows trampled on it and wasted it.

The fence changed all that. Separated from the haycrop, the lower slope's fresh green grass became the next course in the stirks' diet after they had eaten off the calf field.

That Sunday saw the practice put in motion for the very first time. Gordon and Robert hammered in metal supports, threaded wires that would carry the current and set the big yellow battery a'ticking. Then in a combined family operation we rounded up Jasper, Erik the Red, Frances, Charles and Caroline and, after precautiously barricading off possible escape routes, drove them out of the field, along the narrow lane between our house and the orchard, through the beck and up the cart-track to the top gate. We crossed the road in a bunch and shut the gate behind the animals who were now safely contained in that bottom piece of the Scar field.

We couldn't believe it. No one broke away in the wrong direction. No one jibbed at the beck and there was not so much as a pushbike to cause confusion on the road. It wasn't like us at all.

The next similar exercise was though. It took place some weeks later after Jasper and company had eaten off the grass and been sold at Malton market.

Now *that* was the part of cattle rearing we always hated. Parting with animals we had known since knock-kneed babyhood was a downright miserable affair. The only faint consolation to us was that they were store cattle—not destined for immediate slaughter but with a few more months of grazing on better pasture than we could provide; muddled thinking undoubtedly.

It was a good market. The beasts commanded a decent price—but so did the six two-week old calves Gordon bought in their place.

'What sort of calves shall I buy?' Gordon had teased Roger before he left for Malton.

Roger, an independent thinker, had suggested a yellow one. And that is how a Charolais came to join the herd, her sandy-beige colouring being the closest to yellow available that day.

She was a raving beauty. She was also, in my opinion, raving mad. I was feeling pretty much the same way myself when, after a fortnight's intensive persuasion, perseverance and perspiration on my part she had not, so far as I could see, absorbed a single drop of nourishment.

By this time I had had a fair bit of experience at teaching calves to drink from a bucket. Aberdeen Angus calves are notoriously slow to get the hang of it and our cows had been mostly bred to Angus but, compared with the

Charolais, they were jet-propelled. She was dumb—utterly clueless.

The French Faggot, as Binnie named her, believed it was sufficient simply to stand around fluttering her beautiful long eyelashes and looking glamorous. Doing anything so intelligently advanced as swallowing was completely beyond her. I spent hours in that pen trying to teach her to suck my fingers. The only successful session took so long that the milk had cooled and as her nose encountered it she was so electrified that we both nearly hit the roof.

I fixed a black lamb teat to a plastic orange-squash bottle and tried to squeeze milk between her clenched jaws. I pushed the teat between her lips in the corner of her mouth and the milk ran straight out the opposite side. It was, sighed the French Faggot faintly, rolling her eyes in a very continental manner, too *much* pour pauvre petite elle.

Daily, my drink-this-up-for-mummy smile deteriorated as the skin of the backs of my fingers wore off on a row of strong incisors and lovely nourishing milk ran everywhere except down the inside of Charolais' throat. One way or another milk was being thrown away like dishwater.

In the space of minutes Roger accidentally knocked over a two-gallon pailful that I was about to take out to the other calves. A Dinky toy which he and Antony were squabbling over dropped into the second, spraying milk like a geyser right up the kitchen window, and as I was going outside with the remainder the door handle hooked into my sleeve and I dropped the lot.

I charged into the Charolais' pen waving the bottle and yelling, 'If you don't drink it this time, you old faggot, I'll *hit* you with it.' And with a genteel shudder—whether because of the milk or my manners I neither knew nor cared—she drank it down like a lady.

Of the other bought-in calves only Sarah stands out in memory because she is still around somewhere, the mother now of many a fine calf but a terror of the first water.

We ought to have been warned how she would develop

when, as Gordon opened the back doors of the Morris Traveller she—a two week old black and white Hereford heifer—stepped out with such self-possession, and without any prompting marched straight to the pen allotted her. With fastidiously wrinkled nostrils she closely examined it. Yes, she said, with a few minor adjustments which she would see to herself, this would be quite satisfactory. We bowed ourselves out from the presence. She became a great crony of Snowdrop's which, as *she* turned out, was inevitable.

For a while nine calves occupied the pens in the farmyard but came the day when five of them were promoted to the freshly-grown grass of the calf field. In our first year, following the example of Westwath's previous owner, we had run each beast separately on a halter on a short cut through the garden—still a courtesy title in those days. But there was a tendency for the leader to run round one side of trees and the led round the other, with the resulting confusion lasting until teatime.

If this disadvantage had not become apparent I should have vetoed the practice anyway because I had lost no time in carving from the wilderness a proper garden where this sort of bullrush was out of place. So, although it was a longer way round, during succeeding years the calves were driven en bloc to their destination through the back fields. It was when we did the same thing that year that things took on a familiar aspect.

It began the moment we opened the calf pen doors. There we were, Gordon, Robert, Antony, Jess and I, manning strategic positions, briefed and ready to spring into action and channel the animals straight into the field. There were the doors standing invitingly wide and clear. And there inside were five firmly planted beasts refusing point-blank to come out at all.

Even when Antony went inside and smacked Blackie's bottom the calf only circled around and around, passing the gaping doorway as if it was sealed by an invisible ray. Snowdrop took it further. She was a *good* girl, she said smugly. She knew she wasn't allowed out there. Self-righteously she stood well back from her doorway.

Sarah, typically, sparked off the trouble. Craftily she waited until Antony moved in behind her then, like a greyhound released from the trap, shot off down the farmyard.

She had chosen her moment well because by this time most of the sentries had left their posts. I, for one, was striding peremptorily to the scene of the hold-up, pertinent questions ready on my lips.

The sad truth was, only Jess was still at her station and that solely because she had unearthed from beneath the hen-house an old bone, so even *her* mind was off the business in hand. Blissfully gnawing, her eyes cocked heavenwards, she got the shock of her life when Sarah passed her going like Red Rum. Jess grabbed her bone and also went off like Red Rum—though in a different direction. She threw us a defiant look as she sped past. Had to knock off now, she said. It was Saturday. We saw her next at teatime.

That moment Blackie and Alexander erupted into the yard. If they had taken the same route as Sarah it would not have been quite so chaotic, which was the very reason why they didn't. And while we were all rushing about shouting unheeded instructions and blaming each other, Snowdrop, finding that she was playing to an empty house and that virtue didn't pay anyway, emerged suddenly from purdah and knocked a water-trough for six. Last seen, she was making off down the holme field jumping off all four feet at once.

One thing living at Westwath did for us—it kept us in good physical trim. Jogging wasn't much heard of in those days but *had* anyone suggested such a thing we should have laughed him to scorn. Olympic standard sprinting we may have considered.

We sprinted then, that hot afternoon in early summer.

Antony was the luckiest. Fortuitously his quarry, Nicholas, ran the correct course across the hayfield and straight through the calf field gateway. Antony victoriously shook hands with himself and went off to help Robert with Alexander.

He had *had* to shut the gate, to keep Nicholas *in*, Antony explained indignantly, when I turned up later with Blackie to find myself stymied again.

It wasn't as if I hadn't already known suffering. I had only got that far owing to bribery and that, I thought bitterly, wasn't going to stand me in good stead much longer. I had caught Blackie's attention by waving a bucket of nuts under his nose as he galloped past, and led him to the gate by setting off quickly in the right direction without letting him put his head in the bucket. Unfortunately there were only two nuts remaining in it. I lost the others when the back field fence collapsed beneath me. My shin, streaming blood, was very sore.

I dropped the bucket and tore at the gate. It was the usual kind of farm gate—it opened quite wide if you lifted it, turned it and dragged it properly. Unhappily, as I yanked at it the top bar lifted completely off and fetched me a fourpenny one right across the nose.

Through a curtain of blood I discerned Gordon canter past hanging on to Snowdrop's tail. His face turned white as a sheet when he caught sight of mine.

'Are you all right?' he called fatuously, disappearing suddenly with his gorgeous girl friend into a ditch.

Life, as I remarked before, had returned to normal.

9

Going batty

We were into haytime. Will Arrowsmith had been with the cutter and grass lay in long, neat, eau-de-nil coloured rows ready for turning. We were having an abnormally hot spell and mercury was already soaring in the thermometer as, early in the morning, I mounted the stone steps to the hayfield. All day I walked along between the rows swinging the wooden rake to the farther side and pulling over the swathes, seed-head first, to expose the underside to the sun. By lunchtime the thermometer propped by the top step registered 108°F. I pointed it out to George, the Calor gas man, who happened to arrive with new cylinders just then, and we each shook both the thermometer and our heads. Fancy, we said, who would have believed it!

Well I would, for one. After lunch I stripped off down to shorts and the top piece of my swimsuit, secure in the knowledge that in our secluded back hayfield no one could possibly see me.

That was the signal for people to appear as if summoned by bells. The first to arrive was Mary Stewart with my little god-daughter. She laughed so much she could hardly hold the baby. She placed her in the shade of a bush and composed herself sufficiently to seize a spare rake and walk the rows with me. We turned hay as we talked and in a very short time Mary saw the advantage of my skimpy clothing.

As Mary and Tracey departed, Will's wife and sister arrived. They, too, had a tendency to fall about. You would have thought, I said huffily, they had never seen anyone in a swim-suit before. If this was the effect my figure had on everyone I was thankful my visitors were all female.

Far above, in the Ellers Farm field beyond the wood, haymaking was in progress also. I could plainly hear the tractor and when it drove along the nearer side, could glimpse the driver's head and shoulders between the trees. The distance was too great to make out whether it was Charlie or Tom and I was confident that he could distinguish me no more clearly, and so wouldn't hurt himself laughing.

Day after day I toiled alone in the field—it was an abnormally heavy crop. Straight after school Robert, Antony and Pauline—Will's and Joan's daughter who was an indispensable part of our haytime—relieved me while I milked and prepared a meal. Gordon, hurrying home from work, weighed in the moment he arrived. We all suffered with sunburn, blistered hands and exhaustion.

Then suddenly we were shoved another step forward into the age of the machine. Pauline arrived with a message from Tom up at Ellers farm—we could, if we liked, have the borrow of their aud hay-to'nner . . . they'd gotten a new 'un.

I was delighted. Gordon went up straightaway with our tractor and came clattering back with the turner. Tom, Gordon said, had told him we were welcome to it. He had also told him he couldn't watch the missus sweating her guts out like that . . . I reeled and went to put on a shirt, but thought it was the nicest thing I had ever heard.

From then on my life improved. We actually bought the hay-turner—quite cheaply because it lacked a few tines and things—but to me it was a gift from heaven. Gordon or Robert drove the tractor and turned and windrowed the hay in only a fraction of the time it had taken to do it by hand. And to gild the gingerbread Will offered to bale it for us.

Excitement mounted to fever pitch that day. The boys'

selfless offer to stay home from school to help was turned down. Roger and I paced up and down with anxious eyes on the sky where a small cloud was hesitating and cocked eager ears for the sound of Will's tractor.

He came at half past two in the afternoon driving insouciantly down our rough steep track, making the sharp right-angled turn on to the wath as unconcernedly as if there had been acres to play about in instead of inches, proceeding across the beck with an unworried backward glance at the baler whose wheels actually protruded for half their width over either side of the concrete wath, on between the stone gateposts—I covered my eyes, suddenly aware that the opening was too narrow and Will hadn't a chance of getting through ... or of turning around to go back—and when I opened them the whole caboodle was swinging into the yard.

Will was grinning from ear to ear. Thowt he wasn't going to mek it, he announced cheerfully, taking a turn through the back field gate on his way to the hayfield.

It took just over an hour for the machine to thump out one hundred and eighty-eight bales and all I had to do was encircle the field pulling in the loose stuff from the edges into the baler's path.

'Let's get it led before Dad comes home,' cried Robert, dashing home from school and changing into jeans.

'Leading' your hay is not like leading a horse, say. You actually pick up the hay and carry it to wherever you want to store it, so now I rocked on my heels. It was a revolutionary idea and, for a moment, quite beyond my imagination. But we were lucky in every way. That week the holiday bungalow was occupied by a wonderful couple from Withernsea, and without any ado Mr Richardson rolled up his sleeves and went around the field stacking the bales, which were exceptionally heavy ones according to Will, into manageable cubes.

Robert uncoupled the turner from the tractor and replaced it with the sledge. I made air-shafts in the hayshed—standing long lengths of timber on end in threes like long, narrow tepees tied by their tops to the roof beams—and after milking and giving the calves their tea (we hadn't time for ours) went to help the others—Mr Richardson, Pauline, Robert and Antony—who had already led many of the mini-stacks.

When Gordon came home it was all finished.

I can see him now, wearily mounting the hayfield steps, coming to a thunderstruck halt at the edge of the empty field, one hand to the back of his head, his drawn face lighting with laughter as the meaning of the sight sunk in.

It was one of the more satisfying moments of life.

But we were far from done yet. There were still the top fields across the road to tackle. With the electric fence removed, the shorn bottom and long growth on top endowed the Scar field with the appearance of a pudding-basin haircut.

Then Will returned with the mower and off we went again.

This time there would be no baling. Those fields were too steep even for Will. The turner was worth its weight in gold, lifting and raking, letting in air and sunlight until the once lush grass dried out and became hay, but it could not carry the process through to its conclusion and make bales. The hay still had to be piled into cocks by hand and led down to the farmyard in loose mounds. Never had there been such a heavy crop. The whole field lay under a deep quilt of it, each row overlapping the next.

Then the weather turned against us and it couldn't have been more contrary had it tried.

First a searing hot gale sprang up rolling the loose hay into writhing ropes, tearing off the tops of cocks and sending them spinning over the wall to bounce lightly far away over the heather. Then, with the hay biscuit-dry and the sledge grinding its way up for the first load, the sky tore apart with a brilliant rip-roaring crash releasing water of a volume equal to the capacity of Lake Windermere.

Squelching up and down the field in wellingtons a couple of days later, stabbing into mounds of stuff so saturated that when I tried to lift it the fork bent like a fishing rod, I mused on life and its inconsistencies. Rain, I knew, was necessary to life but why the blue, blacking and matches (my mother's favourite oath, that one) it had to come *after* the wind, I couldn't think.

Sheer contrariness, of course, the same reason that Storky had her kittens on a pile of logs out in the comfortless woodshed when I had already prepared a nice warm wool-lined nest in the kitchen for her.

All the cats were being particularly assertive just then. Charlotte, Storky's mother, had given birth to a kitten at two o'clock in the morning in Robert's bed while Robert was in it. Because of Robert's loudly expressed objections Gordon had got up and removed mother and child to the kitchen; and we had just recovered from that when Butterscotch had her babies in the attic. It was her scratching about as she made up a bed in a carton of *Farmers Weeklys* that wakened us. We thought at first it was rats.

The next night we were wakened not by cats or rats. It was (would you believe it?) bats.

To begin with I thought it was a moth that fluttered about the room and I sleepily blew out the little paraffin kelly lamp to foil a possible suicide attempt.

The fluttering continued. It sounded like a very *big* moth. After a few moments of conjecture I lighted the lamp again. That was a mistake. The flapping shadow thrown across the ceiling was enormous.

I gave Gordon an urgent dig in the ribs. 'Wake up,' I said. 'We've got a visitor.'

Gordon groaned. 'Oh no, not again. Who is it this time?'

'I rather *think* it's Dracula.'

The sash window was lowered a couple of inches. The creature had had no difficulty flying in through *that* and you would have expected that when Gordon lowered the sash to the limit and flung open the casement on the opposite wall so that there were apertures of about eighteen square feet, all told, it could have found its way out again with even less trouble. But no.

Obviously sharing with the rest of the animals on the place the superstitious belief that it was unlucky to go out the same way as you came in, it was determinedly trying to bash its way through a wall two feet thick.

Following Gordon's instructions I shone the torch straight on to it to make it believe, Gordon said, it was daylight. When I dutifully enquired the reason for this my husband explained kindly that if it was daylight the bat would stop flying. Sure enough, a few minutes later the bat did stop flying and clung to a flower on the wallpaper, though whether he really did think it was daylight or had merely knocked himself silly I wouldn't pontificate.

Gordon plucked him from the wallpaper and placed him outside sadly advising him that the landlady had said definitely *no* pets.

Dracula became a regular visitor, however, finding his own way in and—after that first night—out, until I tacked a piece of net curtaining over the window opening.

It was not that I was inhospitable, I told him, but I did need some *sleep*.

10

Cat-astrophe

It was weariness that caused me to yawn so much, not boredom. Boredom never gave any of us a moment of concern, which was more than could be said for other factors. The cats, for instance. There were four of them at that time, a colourful lot in both senses.

Charlotte was pink and blue and given to swearing. Snapping her toe-pads at the commonly held conviction that all ginger cats are toms, she saddled us with two uncompromising ginger females, both, while kittens, alike as two peas. As they grew older differences became apparent but by then they had been named Stork and Butter developing in the course of time, to Storky and Butterscotch.

Later, Charlotte had a son and to confound the pundits thoroughly he wasn't ginger at all but an unblemished grey-blue. Except when bathed in sunlight—when he irradiated silver. Smudge was a gentle lad with enormous soulful eyes and we did not have him neutered in the hope he would keep the girls at home.

Butterscotch was almost totally deaf though she could hear very high notes like whistles or hisses. Her amber eyes were soft and peered anxiously about her as if expecting to be ambushed by bandit cats at any moment. Her movements were exaggeratedly cautious and the sight of her tiptoeing about and craning her head around corners unsettled us as well. We would go over and look round the corner to see what was drawing her and she would be so startled at us appearing suddenly at her shoulder that she would leap a foot in the air and scare us out of our wits.

When she wasn't gliding around wringing her hands like the Grey Lady she would be on the sideboard, front paws up on the top of mother's black marble clock peering yearningly into the room through the mirror. Or, as a change from being Alice, she would set up a Punch and Judy Show on the kitchen window sill. On the outside, pleading to be let in, she ran her front paws from side to side along the lowest horizontal bar of the sash window like a feline Chopin, her hind feet quite stationary. Usually some of her relations were also on the sill, sitting upright with dreamy-eyed patience, until Butter, playing a twiddly bit at the top end of the keyboard, impinged on their airspace. Then the relative most affected would fetch her a back-hander, she retaliated with a hook to the jaw, somebody else would swipe the fourth who, until that moment had been innocently unaware of anything untoward. He would fall off the sill and disappear from our view followed by Butter who had lost her balance, leaving the other two glaring at each other thoroughly affronted.

Storky had a twirl of fur on the nape of her neck—the result of excessive transportation by her mother. We used to think sometimes that Charlotte was a frustrated chess champion.

Storky differed from her sister in other ways, too. Where Butterscotch drooped and dreamed, Storky was alive and vital, her jewel-green eyes alight with intelligence.

Not for Storky a long patient wait on the windowledge. If admittance wasn't immediately forthcoming she opened the window herself—from the top. A vertical jump, claws grappling the upper frame, a hefty swing, and the next second a ball of ginger fur exploding on the table scattering cornflakes right, left and centre. Many a night we were galvanized by the rumble of the descending window into burglar repelling stations only to meet on our cautious descent to the kitchen the coldly enquiring stare of Storky interrupted in mid-wash.

Disconcerting though this was to us, it was nothing to the impression made on visitors who—with a wondering eye on one cat standing on a clock and trying to get into a mirror—were sipping tea and asking if we didn't feel bored with so little happening in the country, when another, apparently air-borne cat, catapulted into their laps.

Even the window itself looked peculiar. Not only were the three bottom panes permanently opaque with muddy footprints but, thanks to Storky, seven feet up from ground-level the top panes were similarly impressed.

It was Storky's intelligence that was responsible for her babies being born in the woodshed. Her first one born in the house had mysteriously disappeared, hadn't it? So had Charlotte's. So had Butterscotch's. Therefore when one morning she came home with a new slim figure and a smug expression we knew just how her mind had been working. I ran the four kittens to ground in a strawy nest among the logs and was relieved and delighted to see that one of them was pink and blue like its Grannie. That one was guaranteed a home.

Later that afternoon the woman who had requested it happened to call and I led her to the hut to view the goods. They weren't there. There wasn't a sign of a kitten ever having been there—nor the slightest indication where they had gone.

Storky when confronted looked surprised, said, 'What kittens?', had her tea and vanished.

She appeared again the next morning for breakfast and, attaching myself to her like a police tail, I followed her down the garden when she went out. We strolled together down the path—she having companionably waited for me to catch up. She was going to sit on the wall in the sun for a bit, she confided, seeing there was nothing *urgent* to attend to.

I watched her reclining there like an abandoned Davy Crockett hat for ages and the second I turned away to go and wash the milking buckets she vanished again. We saw her only at mealtimes and always afterwards she gave us the slip.

For days the whole family searched for kittens. It became obsessional. Mother would suddenly leave the washing-up to look into the fuel store. Gordon would come home, after chewing the problem over all day at the garage, walk straight past the house and poke in the calf field hayrack. The boys and I had investigated the garden hut, the potting-shed, the old Robin's Nest, the hut in the calf field, the workshop and the hayshed.

The hayshed was an obvious first choice but this year, owing to the heavy crop, the place was jammed solid to the roof. There wasn't a chance of anything hiding in it. There was even an overflow stack of hay under a tarpaulin in the yard and we searched that thoroughly, too.

Occasionally Storky would materialize beside us and peer interestedly into corners with us, sometimes helpfully poking in an exploratory paw and tut-tutting sympathetically when we found nothing there and screamed at her.

The truth was our nerves had worn threadbare. For six weeks we had been going round like a spy-ring... shadowing Storky every time she left the house—and she rarely went twice in the same direction. Gum-shoeing down the path, darting between buildings and looking furtively around corners. Bungalow tenants were electrified when, in mid-sentence and for no apparent reason, we left them to lope on tiptoe across the yard, drop suddenly to our knees and peer under the hen house. They thought we were mental. It didn't help either when Storky backed out from underneath and looked at us with the same expression. She didn't know we were interested in mousing, she said.

And so the weeks passed without us catching sight of so much as a kitten's whisker. We knew by the appearance and feel of Storky's undercarriage that she was still feeding them and made sure she had extra rations of food to keep up her strength. Then one evening she did not appear for tea.

I hadn't seen her at breakfast nor—I realized with a shock—the evening before. Not, in fact, since the previous morning when she had walked over to the road to see mother and me off to the village when Binnie called for us in her car.

With growing alarm I scoured the roadside verges for half a mile in each direction in case she had been hit by a car. There was nothing. We searched the farm in case she had accidentally been locked in somewhere—all the nooks and crannies we had poked during the kitten hunt were looked at again. The little straw nest in the woodshed was a pathetic reminder of the plight of the babies should anything have happened to their mother. I felt sick with worry.

I broke off searching at last because milking was long overdue. Jess ran into the holme field and brought home the cows. Miserably I swung the chains around their necks pushing the metal toggles through the rings, turned to lift stool and bucket off the low wall and nearly dropped both.

Storky—a dishevelled, agitated and talkative Storky—was bounding through the doorway. Relief flooded over me like a tide as I swept her into my arms. But that was not what she wanted. She struggled down and ran across to the hayshed. Clinging halfway up the wall of hay she turned and fixed me with her green eyes, calling urgently with her funny cracked voice. Then, because I was too stupid to understand, jumped down with a sinuous twist, ran towards me a little way, turned and sprang up the hay again.

At long last the penny dropped. 'They *can't* be up there,' I said disbelievingly. In answer she threw me an old-fashioned look, squirmed up under the narrow canopy on the shed roof and disappeared. The hay sprang back and sealed her entry place as if it had never been.

'Not in the *hay*,' said Antony when my shouts drew him over. 'She couldn't get in!'

She had though, I told him. And when we had pulled out half the side of the stack, there she was at the top of one of the air shafts I had made with the poles. She was tearing frantically at the hay, only pausing to natter over her shoulder to tell us to hurry up and help her dig.

'They must be down *there*,' Antony cried, 'but a lot of hay's fallen in. We'll have to pull it all out..!'

Between us we dragged out masses and masses of the stuff. It expanded and grew like candy-floss. We passed it behind us and it filled the yard between the shed and cowhouse. It was like digging a tunnel out of Colditz.

Storky, mopping her brow, stopped digging to crane her neck down the excavation and chatter encouragement. From her point of view it wasn't so much like Colditz as an incident in the Blitz. I could just see her passing down cups of tea, leading a morale-boosting chorus of 'Roll Out the Barrel' and expecting a medal for it in the end. Just as if she wasn't the cause of all the trouble in the first place.

The kittens could be heard now. Muffled squeaks came from a position well down inside the shaft which was now cleared of the blockage. With a cry of victory Storky dived inside, reappearing briefly to give us a curt nod of dismissal.

'Didn't you get them out?' asked Gordon later that evening when we related the story, marvelling how Storky had hauled four babies, one by one, over a distance of fifty yards from log hut to hayshed involving scaling a four-foot high, pointed-paling gate and climbing up to the top of, then down inside, a twelve-foot haystack without any of us spotting her. Then never once letting herself be seen in the vicinity afterwards until that day when, because of all the times she had scrambled in and out, the hay had caved in and trapped them all.

And *then*, I said fondly, having the sense to lead me to the scene.

'Yes,' said Gordon patiently, 'but didn't you get them *out*?'

No, we hadn't got them out, I said. But at least we now knew where they *were*. Thereby proving myself wrong again. Because when we all trooped down to demonstrate the whys and the wherefores and, puzzled by the utter silence, cleared out the shaft to the *empty* nest . . .

Gordon gave me his droopy-eyed Robert Mitchum look and went in to his supper.

11

Facts of life

Luckily, I found the kittens the next day. I was broodingly shovelling dairy nuts out of bins in the doghouse when, from the calfpen next door, I thought I heard a faint squeak. Antony and I cautiously peeped inside. The pen contained no calves at that time but was, like every available space, stuffed full of hay and in it, dancing about as if on a trampoline, were the four well-grown kittens. This time Storky had contrived, carrying kittens weighing about a pound and a half each, to jump up a door as high as my shoulder and in through an aperture barely large enough to admit herself.

Antony and I rounded them up with hardly less trouble than if they'd been calves and carried them to the kitchen, setting them round a saucer of milk. Storky arriving a few minutes later and sizing up the situation, went out and returned almost immediately with a mouse. The kitchen, she announced blatantly, was where she'd intended them to be all the time. On the chair in the warm corner by the Rayburn. And that is where two of them grew up.

The other two went to good homes. The pink and blue one's owner later reported that hers wouldn't drink milk from a bottle. She had to warm it first and pretend it was straight from the cow. The pretty sandy-beige one went to our butcher to be, Gordon said, made into pork pies.

The remaining pair we called the Banderlog, the monkey-people, because that is what they looked like with coats mottled grey, ginger, beige and black. One was more black than the other and their names became simplified to Dark Bundy and Light Bundy or, collectively, the Bundies. They spent most of their time up the apple trees seeing how far out along the thinnest branches one could push the other before she fell off.

The Wards returned for their summer visit and as they arrived the kitchen door dropped off its hinges—which prophesied no good. So Gordon blamed them, too, when on his way home from work that day the car's suspension broke and he drove all the way at five miles an hour with it tied up with binder twine (see Chapter 4).

However I was willing to forgive them everything because I needed their help to further a project I had in mind. I called it, grandly, my riverside terrace garden.

All my life I had wanted a waterside garden and here we were with this beautiful beck passing only yards from the front of the house and separated from it by an elongated triangle of rubbish known, euphemistically, as the low orchard. This is what I was determined to clear and terrace, and when better to start than now with the Wards' visit coinciding with the first week of Gordon's summer holiday from the garage? Consequently, Denis and Gordon were organized into a tree-felling, digging-out and sawing-up party while I stood around and directed like Capability Brown, Percy Cane and Gertrude Jekyll rolled into one . . . Tiring, I found it.

The fatigue even spread to the orchard wall which collapsed in a heap of rubble under our front window and Gordon, faced with a formidable dry stone walling job, hurriedly had a splendid idea and said he had always thought that a pair of wrought iron gates would look good just there. And so—when Binnie produced a pair out of thin air—they did.

All too soon the Wards' holiday ended. It was the last day, also, for Barbara and Judy Bruce, mother and daughter, whose stay in the bungalow coincided as usual with our friends' holiday. Judy joined Janet, David and our own three boys for the customary last night feast in the Robin's Nest—a tradition that was to be unbroken for almost a decade and reluctantly terminated due only to the participants' advancing staid maturity.

That particular evening concluded with a ceremony fittingly performed in the beck.

You see, I was not the only one held in thrall by the beck. All the children who ever stayed at Westwath have been. Swimming in it, canoeing on it, damming it, building cairns in it. This year's cairn had been an ambitious one with a lantern top containing a candle and called 'the lighthouse'. The actual lighting of it was saved for the last evening.

We who survive will always remember that summer night. The golden candle-light spilling over into the shallow water so that the ripples appeared to be bubbling ready-gilded from some underground Aladdin's cavern. Water noises accentuated by darkness... plops which tell of water voles... clop, clops sounding like hoof-beats that can only be the passing of Pan ... upriver the *quack*, quack, quack of a mallard who saw him go. Children's shouts and laughter, we older ones' more subdued remarks, and around us the warm, scented fathomless night.

The children still come back to the beck—the married ones bringing spouses—one is now at university, another at college and Antony is in the RAF. With Antony's proneness to accidents I fear the country is taking a big risk, there.

So were the scouts from my old group in Hull when, the next week, they invited Antony to camp with them. They had rented a super waterside site at a farm a couple of miles up the road. For ten years I had been Cubmaster to the group and the present Scoutmaster—this dates me all right—was one of my old cubs.

After Antony had been in camp three days Maurice, the Scouter, called, as he happened to be passing, to pick up Antony's sponge-bag which, he said apologetically, I had forgotten to pack.

I jolly well *had* packed it, I told him firmly.

And so I had. When Antony returned at the end of a blissful week there it was, dry and pristine, at the bottom of the kitbag where I had put it.

It didn't matter, Antony said airily. He hadn't needed it. He had fallen off the aerial runway into the beck three times.

While Antony was in camp our annual load of straw was delivered. We rather hoped that he and the rest of the scouts would drop by because extra help is always welcome on these occasions. Though that year, for the first time, we were spared the chore of leading it piecemeal down the cart-track from its usual delivery site up the road by the Browns' house because Gordon had asked Geo Carter to unload it in the garage field as close to the end of the wath as possible.

In case anyone is puzzled why Geo did not drive straight over the wath (and if there is still somebody who doesn't know what a wath is, I'll tell you: it's the Old Norse word for 'ford') I must point out that this is Westwath and pretty much as some Old Norseman left it.

There are two means of access to the wath on the outer, field side. There is the track leading down from the top gate, which is too narrow, too rough, too steep and too tree-overhung for a waggon carrying a towering, four-and-a-half-ton load of straw to negotiate, and there is a little path leading straight out of the field which is too narrow, too rough, too steep and too tree-overhung for *anything* to negotiate, except on foot.

I kept well out of the way while the unloading was going on. Last year, when Geo and I had unloaded and restacked it all on our own, was yet a vivid memory.

Gordon was still home on holiday—Robert was there, too . . . I reckoned the three of them could do without me so I turned a deaf ear to the arrival of the waggon and took myself to lighter, or anyway, more interesting work in my new river-garden.

The terrace was coming along nicely now. I had levelled the bank and was building a retaining wall using soil instead of mortar and inserting rock plants at intervals as I went along. Before lunchtime that day I put in two more courses and, as usual, got as much soil and compost in my hair as between the stones. This happened because we were designated as a low flying area. Every time a plane screamed overhead I clapped my hands to my ears. More often than not I was carrying a bowl of soil or manure...

I was very surprised to learn that the straw had been delivered and was even now awaiting leading into the yard, and magnanimously offered—because, try as I would I could think of no excuse that would hold water—to lend a hand.

The old sensation as I was introduced to the mountain of bales was like a knife turned in the stomach. Because it was intended to move the bales on into the farmyard immediately, they had been indifferently stacked and seemed spread out over half the field. With a pessimistic eye on the weather someone had thrown a plastic sheet over which protected, perhaps, a tenth of it. For some reason, no doubt psychological and connected with my muddy hair, the scene reminded me of the aftermath of a plane disaster.

The pessimist had been right about the weather. No sooner was the sledge loaded with the first dozen bales than a light drizzle began. The sledge was actually a piece of old carpet, a brainwave of Gordon's when at the fifty-ninth second we remembered that the proper one was in need of repair. (The proper one had had a previous life as a very solid oak and iron bed-base.)

Gordon, Robert, Roger, Alison—a little girl who was staying in the bungalow—and I worked like fury carrying bales down the short path and stacking them on the sledge where it lay behind the tractor on the wath. Then they were towed across and up into the yard where we all went frantic trying to find sheltered places to stow them. The hay in the barn had settled a bit by then and it was surprising how many bales we found room for on top of it. It surprised me, anyway, who was up there under the roof on the receiving end. It uncomfortably brought to mind a medieval torture I had once read about and, ever since, tried to forget. I imagined that when the bales were removed next winter all that would be found of me would be a smear of pulp.

When the hayshed definitely would hold no more we scurried about poking odd bales into corners of buildings like squirrels hiding nuts. Before we were half done the drizzle turned to fine, steady rain. Mother would never have recognized her carpet. It was all one with the muddy yard. All of us—including little Alison who from all appearances was enjoying the holiday of her life—were soaked to the skin.

My trouser hems became so waterlogged and heavy that they dragged under my feet and were trodden into the mud. The weight of *that* pulled the trousers down even more and, for the rest of the afternoon, at one-minute intervals, I was hoisting them up from around my knees.

For some reason none of us felt like pulling out a piece of straw and lolling on a gate to chew it.

The sun came out as we finished, and a couple of scouts arrived.

While the Scouters were stuck with Antony, we played hosts to their boys who came in twos and threes to camp overnight in the corner of one of our fields—the culmination of a long hike which was part of their badge work. On the whole, it was a fair exchange.

Town lads, they all loved to stand in the cool, dim cowhouse to watch me milk—and even try their hand at it. That was fine with me. They liked to talk to me about scouting activities and about their homes and families—some of these boys I had taught as tots in Sunday school, so that was fine too.

What I did find heavy going were the questions. Not all of them. I could take things like, What's her name? or, What do you feed 'em on? in my stride. But there are matters with which, quite honestly, I am not equipped to deal.

I had explained to the best of my ability where the milk came from and why, and that Rhoda was producing more than Bluebell because she had calved more recently. And then came the seventy-five thousand dollar question.

'But, where,' asked one small youth, eyes round with genuine innocence, 'does the calf come *out*?'

All right, I defy *you* to do better than I did without previous notice.

'Well,' I said after a long silence while I hoped the roof would fall in or that Rhoda would kick him or something, 'well, from her rear.'

I *knew* it was badly put and I'm sorry for any future confusion I may be responsible for. As the cows filed out of the doorway I was thunderstruck to see the boys peering, with utter amazement, into Rhoda's ear.

12

One blue cow

We were going to a farm sale to buy a cow! This was the day after we had led all that straw, and we felt that a nice relaxing day at the sale would do us and our muscles the world of good. It was a beautiful day, too, all sunny and golden with a little bit of wind, and so first I did the washing. By hand—no electricity you'll remember—for six of us, and pegged it on the line. Gordon and the boys finished clearing up loose straw from broken bales and tidied up the garage field.

Then Gordon and I drove to the next village where the sale was to be held. We hadn't time for a coffee-break so intended merely to have a quick look round, hurry home for an early lunch and return for the commencement of the sale at one o'clock. Nothing ever works out as we plan it. I don't know why we bother.

The carpark field which, when we left the Morris Traveller there twenty minutes before, had contained one other vehicle and a battered enamel bath was, when we returned to it, jam-packed with vans, tractors, cattle-waggons, Landrovers and horse-boxes. The white top of the Traveller was just discernable to a good eye, at the back.

It was obvious, I told my empty stomach, that it was going to have to wait until the end of the sale. When I tell

84

you that the sale-bill comprised a good ten inches of close-set small print, the cows coming up right at the end of the lot, you will have some idea how the news was received.

All our neighbours were there, Will Arrowsmith, the Stewarts, the Hewsons and the Phillipses, all looking well-fed and unfamiliar in their Sunday clothes and without their binder-twine belts.

We did not know the Phillipses very well. They had only recently moved to Rowan Head when Mr Hewson retired and flitted to a neighbouring village. But by the end of that day we had suffered so much together that, like the Old Contemptibles of World War One who endured the horrors of the trenches together, we were held together by a common bond.

The sale began with the contents of the cart shed. We went along with the crowd and stood around while the stuff was brought out and auctioned. There wasn't much of it and certainly nothing that anyone would want to buy so we were rather surprised it took one and a quarter hours to dispose of it.

Not that it wasn't entertaining. If it hadn't been for hunger gnawing at my vitals I should have quite enjoyed it. For country auctioneers are all comedians—I know one who could stand in for Sergeant Bilko and no one the wiser. They believe in audience participation and, being on first-name terms with most of it—the audience, I mean—the performance is a great improvement on the telly. Granted, with items like cattle-clippers, fiddle-drills and snig chains to trot out they have a wider scope. Though I wouldn't recognize a snig-chain if one hung around my neck with a locket on it, I felt more could have been squeezed out of that rather than the pig-trough.

('Come on, George, speak up. Just what tha's bin waiting for. Nay, Bill, tha dissent want it. Tha gitten yan last week. Missus mekkin' Yorkshire pud in it, is she?' Applause and shouts of, 'That's nobbut a bite for Bill.')

At last, the final rusty object of unconjectural function was knocked down to some optimist and we all trooped over to where the bigger implements stood around the perimeter of a small field. They ranged from a couple of tractors through ploughs, harrows, a muck-spreader, cutters, turners, drills down to wheelbarrows, turnip-choppers and peculiar things with tines, hooks and pulleys which could have been used in anything from a munitions factory to an out-of-date veterinary operating theatre. There was also the battered enamel bath speculatively dragged in from the carpark.

Nearly three hours, that lot took. Three hours in which I could feel my insides closing up like a squeezed lemon. I daren't even *think* about a cup of tea. And worse—even surpassing the agonies of hunger—was the torture of nerves.

We had to have that cow. Item number nine on the cattle list . . . 'Blue cow, 2nd calf, served May 31st by Hereford bull'—the only beef cow among a whole tribe of Friesians, Ayrshires, Jerseys and Guernseys. And probably the only one for months to come up for sale while Gordon was so conveniently not at work. I looked round the crowd of smiling faces and imagined that every one of them wanted that cow, and they all looked better able than us to pay for it.

We soon learned of one interested party—Christopher Phillips. We had found ourselves weaving among the implements in the Phillipses' company. Mr Phillips—apparently to his surprise—bought a roller. When I told him I didn't know how he dared bid . . . I was scared stiff just watching, he said he felt the same . . . just look at his legs shaking.

Fellow-feeling led to confidences. We were waiting for the blue cow, we told him. In that case, he wouldn't compete, he said. He was after some other cows, anyway.

After the implements it was the turn of the hay. We read on the sale list there were four hundred and twenty bales of it and my empty tum was convinced that each one would be auctioned separately. It was not so bad as that and we moved on to the sheep. Then the poultry. Then the horses.

And then—oh, the twanging of my nerves—the cattle.

Mr Phillips's knees were trembling. Mine were positively rattling along with my teeth. I had plucked at the inside lining of my jacket pocket until it was in shreds. The remaining threads would have gone, too, if they hadn't slid through fingers slippery with cold sweat.

The first cow, a pretty Jersey, was led out on to the paved yard and was quickly disposed of. Seven more were despatched with equal speed. My state of mind was beyond description and if I read Gordon's pale face correctly, so was his.

Number nine was led out and immediately the atmosphere changed. A quickening of interest rustled through the crowd. My worry mounted. I found it impossible to keep still and paddled around in circles on icy feet, with a nonchalant expression determinedly pinned to my face. On each revolution I absorbed the cow's appearance. A blue cow, she was called, but the blue manifested only as a shading around her head. Otherwise she was pure white. I thought she was really beautiful. If ... *if* we got her, and the likelihood was becoming more remote with each passing second, I should call her 'Heather', I thought.

There was a frightening number of people with designs on that animal. We hadn't dreamed she would be so popular. Voices adding in fives called from many directions. Gordon's was one of them.

On our way to the sale Gordon and I had solemnly agreed that one hundred and twenty pounds was the absolute limit to which we could stretch. And that, indeed, was the peak price paid for items one to eight.

For number nine the bidding shot up, briefly touched one hundred and bounced to a hundred and ten.

I recognized my husband's voice. I stopped gyrating and stared as if mesmerized, which I was.

'Fifteen!'

'Twenty!'

'Twenty-five,' said Gordon defiantly. It was between the

two of them, now. The crowd was as spellbound as I was. It was completely silent for the first time that day.

'Thirty!'

'Thirty-five.' It was the beams and bathroom ceiling again, I acknowledged morosely. Bonkers at last.

I wasn't alone with my opinion. As the next cow was being led out (Friesian, 2nd calf. s. May 25th, Hereford) comments were rumbling around the audience. Whativer would we do wi' her at that price? was the general sentiment.

Later, when we were capable of thought again, we agreed that Gordon *had* done the right thing. We had to have a cow to replace Rosie and it had to be a beef breed. Goodness knew when the chance would come again, and for Gordon to take time off work to go to market would cost a day's pay, adding to the price of the cow, anyway.

(Running ahead with the narrative a little—the cow repaid us handsomely. She supplied us with an exceptionally good calf each year and for her last effort gave us twins. What is more, that sale was one of the last before the price of cattle rocketed, and a hundred and thirty-five pounds for a cow was soon small beer indeed.)

We queued at a little hut to write our cheques. With the receipt we were given the cow's Artificial Insemination certificate. On the dotted line beneath the heading *'Cow's Name'* the word HEATHER stood out in capitals. That clinched it, to my mind. Westwath was meant to have her.

Behind us Christopher and Linda Phillips wrote out their cheque. As well as the roller they had bought a cow, a heifer and two calves. We were all pretty light-headed since released from the tension but when Gordon suggested that, to save transport fees, we join forces and *walk* the animals home, and the Phillipses agreed with alacrity, I had serious thoughts about the height of *their* beams and ceilings, too.

13

The haunting of Heather

The calves were too small for the great cattle drive so Gordon carried them to Rowan Head in the Traveller where they dropped out of the story. And so, I hoped, had I.

After consuming the most enjoyable meal of our lives—ah, yet, I still remember it: hot boiled bacon, new potatoes and peas—I was left at home to do the milking. Linda at Rowan Head, presumably, was similarly occupied. Christopher, Gordon, Robert and Antony put on their cow-poke expressions and headed for what narrowly escaped being the last round-up.

After more than five hours of standing around on legs that kept nagging on about lifting yesterday's straw I was thankful to sink on to the milking stool and rest my head on Bluebell's comfortable corpulence. As the milk thrummed into the pail I talked to its dispensers about the new girl and the amazing coincidence of the name.

I slipped the chains and watched the two cows saunter out into the back field. And that, I mused, was most interesting because, considering their strength of mind and general contrariness, I should have expected they would have made straight for the wath and the garage field. We did not like them to be at the far side of the beck at night in case the water rose while we were asleep and cut them off from the cowhouse, nor did we want them wandering out on to the road. With this one—and one only—fundamental principle they unquestioningly co-operated. It was most peculiar.

They had no such scruples about trooping on to the road in daylight hours. The road led in one direction to Castle Farm where, regrettably, our cows had triumphantly fetched up more than once. This stemmed from the time when Bluebell, failing to become in calf to AI, was taken in desperation to consort with Will's bull. She didn't get in calf by him either but nevertheless, claiming him as her lawful wedded husband, took to marching up the road with an abetting body of her friends and relations to demand resumption of conjugal rights.

Castle Farm exercised an irresistible pull on most Westwath inhabitants. It had been a magnet for our sheep, too, and when its farmyard wasn't milling with Westwath's flock it was acting host to its children. Robert and Antony had played with the Castle Farm youngsters from the beginning and, as a toddler, it was Roger's burning ambition to climb the hill and attain the heights, metaphorically and physically, of Castle Farm. His first extended visit was one Christmastide afternoon when he was two. I collected him after tea. Pauline was being chided by her mother for speaking broad dialect. 'Roger won't understand you. Will you, Roger?'

'Nay,' said Roger, adding his own reproving frown, 'ah weeant.'

I was drawn up there, myself, that evening when all the chores were done. It was half a mile up the road in the direction from which the drovers would be coming. With four miles to walk, they should be appearing there any time now, I reckoned, and I might as well wait for them in the company of Joan Arrowsmith.

At Castle Farm the empty road beyond snaked over the hills. Half an hour and a television programme later it was still devoid of life. I started to worry again and finished off my pocket linings for good and all. The evening wore on. It was a toss-up which would touch bottom first—the sun or my heart—when away on the horizon like an Arab caravan coming over a sand-dune appeared a picturesque little group of men and animals.

It was, I thought romantically and rapidly changing location, such a scene as Constable might have painted. Placid cattle, compliant sheepdogs and contented sons of the soil with the patient philosophy of those who live closely with nature etched deeply on their countenances.

They came nearer. Hurriedly I adjusted my impressions again. Their expressions, I saw, were not so much patient as plain, uncomplicated fed-up.

Oh yes, said Gordon warmly, they had managed very well to start with. Got them rounded up on to the road and up the first hill with no trouble at all. There had been a bit of competition on the straight—the animals being fresh and the men tired—but no trouble to write home about until they got to the stretch where the fence was missing altogether. And—would I believe it? (I nodded vehemently. I would, easily, whatever it was)—a car had driven up, and of all that length of empty road it had chosen to park dead in front of the oncoming animals.

The others finished the story. Not that I needed to hear it. My imagination took over and I saw it all. The cows, excited to begin with by the unusual departure from normal routine, startled by the car coming to a sudden standstill right under their noses, and making off over the unfenced moor like the Calgary stampede with little between the Pennines on one side and the North Sea on the other to stop them. The only bright aspect of the incident to strike me was that I hadn't been part of it.

I was involved in the next episode all right. This was the more painful because I hadn't expected there was to be another episode. How I had read it was—half a mile to home, Heather shunted in with the others. And so to bed . . . flake out . . . finish for the day, praise be.

It wasn't like that at all.

At Castle Farm the ways divided. Christopher and Antony pointed the Phillipses' cow and heifer in the direction of Rowan Head and disappeared down the mile long lane towards it.

Heather, thwarted from following, stood on the crown of the road and gave vent to her feelings in a voice so startlingly high-pitched that our heads rattled. We persuaded her to move in the Westwath direction eventually but it was like being involved in 'Rose Marie'.

'When I'm calling you-oo-*oo*-OO,' bawled Heather.

'. . . answer too-oo-*oo*-OO,' echoed from the Rowan Head lane.

As the distance between us increased, the reply faded away and vanished. Unfortunately this had the effect of making Heather shout louder and, as we proceeded downhill, the walls of the scar threw it back at us. Robert, who had never heard of Rose Marie but who seemed to have caught the atmosphere neatly, said it sounded like a train whistling through the Canadian Rockies, and Heather, who for some yards had been proceeding in roughly the right direction, said she wasn't going down there because of the bears.

We nursed her over that scare and ushered her through the gate into the garage field. Down in our valley it was almost dark. The acres of hanging forest which separated Heather from her friends had swallowed the sun, a slight mist wreathed the pasture and Heather was frightened by a water sprite.

Right on the verge of the wath, we were. Just about to cross. Only yards from the haven of the farmyard when, said Heather, *something* jumped out of the beck and made faces at her. With that she took off like a rocket straight up the cart track and didn't stop until barred by the top gate.

Wearily we climbed up the field to head her off and drove her back to the wath. She did not even pause at the brink but sped by like Pegasus up the minor path into the garage field again, disappearing over a hillock at the lower end.

Down the field pounded Gordon, Robert and I. We rounded up the cow and raced for the wath like Manchester United's forward line . . . and there *they* were, making faces again.

Jess fetched her back this time. The rest of us stood in a row blocking off the way into the field . . . and the next thing we knew there was another way into the field where Heather had veered up the bank and barged straight through a wall. There she stood on an overhanging rock like a Landseer stag, her position emphasizing the obvious fact that her milking was long overdue.

I trailed to the cowhouse for the usual bucket of nuts.

The next period of time—I don't even know how long it was apart from *very* long—passed like many another such at Westwath with people and animals at variance with each other and me scattering nuts as if they were grass seed.

Then some bright spark, obviously at the limit of desperation, suggested roping in Bluebell and Rhoda to help. It might have been a good idea, at that. With the other cows to give her confidence Heather should romp home.

Throughout the whole performance an excited audience of two had been leaning over the back field fence. I let them out into the yard and they followed me eagerly as far as the wath gateway. 'Well, go *on*,' I said.

This was the moment they reverted to character.

Encouraging noises on my part brought horrified stares on theirs. Didn't I know, they reproached me, they weren't *allowed* over there at night? Good gracious, it was *dangerous*. Someone might kidnap them!

It took a great many thumps and shoves before the virtuous creatures reconsidered the position. All right, they would agree to cross so long as it was thoroughly understood that the responsibility was mine. Delicately, they stepped on to the wath.

What with them nervously hesitating, Heather shying at hob-goblins, torchlights flitting about like Will o' the Wisps—Gordon and Robert had the torches, I, to complete the picture of a travelling tinker, was lumbered not only with the bucket but a hurricane lamp—we were all as jumpy as fleas and when Heather, all luminous white, suddenly appeared in front of me from an unexpected direction I dropped the bucket and the last of the nuts rolled into the beck.

At least the girls welcomed each other enthusiatically. It did our hearts good to see it. Now all we had to do was invite all three to run across the wath in a bunch. Bluebell and Rhoda would do it in the customary way, Heather, noting that *they* weren't transported to fairyland, would feel safe to accompany them . . . or be carried across in the rush, anyway, and all three would be in the farmyard before you could say Jack Robinson.

She didn't. She wasn't. They weren't.

At the end of it Bluebell and Rhoda were back in the farmyard all right. Heather was lost in the darkness of the night and the far recesses of the field.

We ran through the whole of the operation twice more with exactly the same result. As I wearily fetched them across the beck again—Rhoda shrugging resignedly, Bluebell turning up her eyes—Christopher and Antony drove up and stopped by the garage. They brought up the numbers on our side to five humans, one dog and— uncertain allies, these—two cows ranged against one lone gremlin-haunted animal.

The outcome was inevitable. Heather won. She did not cross the beck that night.

But we had one minor victory. We milked her. Cornered at last she was haltered and fastened to the top gate. I believe it was Christopher who did the milking . . . I can't remember because I was asleep on my feet. Afterwards we loosed her and left all three cows in the field until morning which was not far off.

Next day, as if she had been doing it all her life, she casually followed the others over the water and sauntered into the cowhouse. All right *now*, she said airily. Naiads weren't active in daytime. Hadn't she noticed me with a bucket of dairy nuts?

14

Duck with sauce

Heather soon settled into our routine. Only once more did naiads raise their heads and this despite its being broad daylight. Coming home with Jess for evening milking Heather relapsed into her old routine at the wath. From a safe distance up the bank she proclaimed that they were watching her again. Blue and Rhoda gave her a look that spoke volumes and turned determinedly in the direction of the beck, unceremoniously scattering any sprites daft enough to be hanging around. Heather, accepting confutation, descended from her refuge, overtook the others by the hen house and was well into her nuts before Bluebell nosed past the door.

We had teething problems, certainly. When, for instance, Heather wanted to stand by the right-hand wall in the cowhouse as she had done at her previous address. The objection to that was black, stubborn and Bluebell-shaped. For nearly fifteen years Blue had rested her tum on that wall and had no intention of making it over to a chalk-coloured soprano who was afraid of fairies. Bluebell was undisputed boss cow in the outfit and Heather, declaring she liked the left-hand wall better, anyway, stepped up into Rosie's old standing.

She did it with a backward stretch of an elegant right leg like a ballerina performing a penché. This strange action,

95

we were to learn, was compulsory and done to appease the spirits. To preserve our shins we used to stand aside until she had got it over with.

That was another thing, Bluebell snorted, plunging her nose into her nuts. Showing off her legs like that. No cow with any self-respect would look so much like a racehorse. Bluebell certainly couldn't be accused of doing that. Her legs were short and thick and clad in sensible black wool.

Heather's legs were so long and her udder so far from the ground that by the time the jet of milk reached the bucket it was reduced to a fine spray and our aim required drastic adjustment.

And there we came to another settling-in complication. Heather would never have countenanced the Sex Discrimination Act. She had never in her life been milked by a woman and wasn't sure it was decent. To make certain it could not happen to her she proceeded, quite literally, to erase me from her life by swinging her body at an angle of forty-five degrees and rubbing me out on the facing wall.

It was a sticky few minutes, I promise you. And threatening to be much stickier. If Gordon hadn't been within earshot all that would have been left of me was an unpleasant smear on the whitewash.

Gordon burst through the doorway as I, trying to get a foothold on Heather's food-trough, was grinding down the wall for the third time. His face, I saw as I rose above Heather's pelvis again, looked shocked. 'Don't shout,' he said. 'You're frightening her.'

'*I'm* frightened,' I yelled. 'Get her off!'

'Poor old Heather,' said my husband soothingly. To me he said, 'Try climbing on to Rhoda's drinking bowl.'

This was something I hadn't thought of but an upward thrust from Heather considerably helped me on my way. I got my feet on to the bowl and teetered there feeling, I must record, very little happier than before because, although I was now out of Heather's range, Rhoda's reaction to this uncventional use of her property was not encouraging. She was tossing her head at me in an uncharacteristically menacing manner . . . and Rhoda was equipped with a pair of forward-curving horns.

It seemed prudent to leave for healthier climes. For my next feat I scrambled on to the wooden partition beyond Rhoda intending to drop in on Bluebell but she, excited by my unexpected appearance over the top and adding her quota of drama, pretended she thought I was a cat-burglar and dared me to go one inch nearer.

To put you out of your suspense I will reveal I did escape with my life. I perched like an eagle on top of the narrow boarding while Gordon unfastened Rhoda and backed her out into the channel. Then he smacked—very non-violently, I noticed—Heather over to her rightful position, and I dropped down into Rhoda's standing and scarpered.

For nearly a week Gordon milked Heather twice daily while I hovered close by and ingratiated myself with her, cooing insincere endearments and daringly scratching her neck. It worked. The next time I sat beside her on the three-legged stool she accepted me without comment and progressed so far as to milk better for me than anyone. Which only went to prove what he'd been telling me, said Gordon. How much she needed friends.

After all that business plus a couple of days spent reroofing the Robin's Nest and the hen and duck-houses, plus—the very day after I washed the walls and ceiling—sweeping the kitchen chimney, Gordon looked forward with relief to the prospect of returning to work.

Anticipation was as far as he got, because that night he stood heavily on a rusty nail, and once more we had the doctor and the vet walking self-consciously up the path together.

The vet, unfortunately, was unable to save the little calf for which we had paid twenty pounds the week before, but Gordon's foot got better just as he developed a mysterious allergy similar to one that had flared up years ago in Hull. Despite visits to a consultant and numerous tests the source of it wasn't discovered then, just as it wasn't this time.

There he was covered, then, from head to the soles of his feet with painful red weals which, I comforted him, at least had the compensating effect of decently hiding the patches of ringworm he had contracted from the calves (everybody's cattle seemed to have it that year). It didn't quite camouflage the hydra-headed carbuncles erupting on his forearm, though.

Lying in bed (he couldn't stand because of blisters on his feet) he nattered about all the jobs he ought to have been doing until this throat closed up and he couldn't speak at all.

He'd got tonsillitis now, said our doctor, wearily descending the stairs again.

Did I think, said a kind elderly lady currently renting the bungalow, as she watched me sorting various pills, lotions and medicines, that my husband was, perhaps, a little run down?

The vet, I said gloomily, would know what ought to be done with him.

The bungalow closed its doors on the last visitor. September drifted into October and I dug potatoes and harvested kidney beans. The only time in years that I could honestly say we *harvested* beans. Every year I sowed them and, if I was lucky, picked enough to fill the original seed packet. The season here is so short with frosts very late and early.

That year was exceptional. We consumed bucketfuls of beans and I prepared and salted down pounds and pounds more in big glass jars. It was a complete waste of time because no matter what I did to them afterwards they proved to be uneatable.

Bird-cherry leaves turned yellow and fell, bowling along the ground on their edges like children's hoops, and drifts of pungent smoke from controlled heather-burning settled in the valley.

Mother, Roger and I had our own blazing bonfires. The garden was being tidied for winter and there were heaps of weeds and briars—stuff too woody for compost—to burn. The fire was covered over each night and stirred into life the following morning. It consumed rubbish that had nurtured and supported our slugs for generations and resulting potash was spread around to enrich our sandy soil.

But it was not so much for the job satisfaction that the occasion was remarkable but for the show-stopping demonstration of mind reading demonstrated by Roger. Such phenomena were not unknown in our family. As a small child Robert had extra-sensory perception to a remarkable degree and had, at times too numerous to be counted, given what proved to be accurate, spontaneous commentaries on happenings out of his physical sight. But for Roger it was unprecedented.

Mother had brought a consignment of brittle brown phlox stems for the fire. 'Do you want this lot?' she asked. 'I think they're all dead.'

They were. Dead as a doornail, like Marley, I thought silently. Immediately Roger looked up from his absorption with the fire. 'Dickens,' he said. 'Who was Dickens, Mummy? Did you know him?'

Roger was four years old and had not, at that time, been introduced to *A Christmas Carol* or, indeed, any other work of Charles Dickens. Nor had I consciously thought of the name, so to call it mind reading is not strictly accurate. Apart from one other instance Roger showed no signs of psychic powers and remains disappointingly normal to this day.

Also normal is the way, with so many mouths to feed already, we attracted so many unprofitable appendages. Antony had a shrewd grasp of the situation. Once when we were moaning about our impecuniosity and wishing we could win the Find the Ball competition, I trotted out the old saying, 'If wishes were horses beggars would ride'. To which Antony replied feelingly, 'If wishes were horses we should have them to feed as well'.

That autumn Wildie moved in with us. She walked up the garden path one morning and stayed for six years.

Wildie was a duck—a mallard—and the trouble with her

was she didn't know she was wild. She didn't consider herself tame, either. She was mistress of herself. She was a duck, she told us simply, who had come to live with us. Preferably in the kitchen where the food was, and *this* would do nicely for a start.

This was in a large dish on the floor and, under the impression that it was *their* breakfast, Storky, Butterscotch, Smudge and the two Bundies radiated from it like a sunburst. Wildie soon put that right. There was going to be a rearrangement round here, she explained through billfuls of cat-food, elbowing her way in and commandeering the whole dish.

The cats fell back in astonishment, too surprised even to object, and sat around in what can only be described as extreme embarrassment.

Smudge, the man of the party and used to the lion's share of whatever was going, crept cautiously forward and put a tentative nose to the dish. This presumptousness was received with a stare so hard that he hurriedly thought better of it and retired to the top of the sideboard where he washed his ears until he got over it. Wildie continued to glare down her bill at the discomforted circle.

Anyone else want to try anything? she hissed, splodging her big feet through the food to retrieve a morsel she had accidentally tossed over the far side. Round-eyed, one and all assured her that they didn't.

Wildie cleared the dish, said it wasn't bad for starters and waddled off down the yard to see what the hens were having.

As the days passed we learned that Wildie preferred layers' pellets to mixed corn. As they were the more expensive, we thought she might. She shovelled them up like a JCB, washing them down with a swig from a muddy puddle.

It had been a muddy puddle only since Wildie's arrival. Before then we had imagined it to be a pan of drinking water for the hens. Wildie preferred to sit on it. At first we demurred. There was the beck, we pointed out. Wildie was firm. She liked to sit on the beck as *well*.

That was why my workload increased to scrubbing out and refilling the pan several times a day instead of once.

Our own resident ducks watched her with horrified admiration. How she *dare*! They had never so much as trespassed in the garden let alone flat-footed it over the doorstep.

This was quite true. The Khaki Campbells had been by far the most well-behaved and least troublesome of all the creatures we had lived with. Reduced in numbers now to the drake and a single duck (retired), they spent their old age dabbling mildly in the beck or sitting side by side like Darby and Joan on the wath.

Regrettably, Wildie's arrival reawakened slumbering emotions in Sir Francis's breast and he began to pursue the lady with a passion unbecoming to one of his years. His wife, Annabelle, dithered in the background and tut-tutted. It turned out, however, that she had no need to worry because Wildie did not feel like *that* about Sir Francis at *all*. Turning the now well-known hard stare on *him* she explained just how things were, and having got that put straight and no hard feelings, said they could tag along with her if they liked.

From then on the three of them were almost inseparable . . . except at the cats' mealtimes which had also become Wildie's. Her main ones, anyway.

They led an idyllic life, these three. All found and nothing whatever to worry about—despite Gordon's heartless habit of hissing 'Green peas', whenever he passed by them. Occasionally, though by no means regularly—she was not going to be taken for granted—Wildie would honour Annabelle and Sir Francis by staying the night with them in their hut though, really, she preferred to be out of doors. A lot of time was spent swimming about the beck, as one would expect, but it was surprising how often the three were to be met in single file on what would seem to be a laborious overland trek through the rushes and long grass at the boggy end of the back fields. From a distance, where only their heads atop long stretched necks could be seen moving above the swaying blades, they looked surprisingly like a fleet of submarines. Especially when they suddenly came into binocular range while we were raking the fields for wild life.

Though why, with wild life's propensity to fasten on to us unbidden, we should actually look for it, I don't know. Perhaps we should have our heads examined.

15

The last straw

Harvest Festival came and went. One of many, I helped dress the church for the event, walking the road to the village beneath arms so full of evergreens I could hardly see over the top. The completed decorations glowed as if lit by a multitude of lamps, the brightness radiating from bonfires of massed chrysanthemums, dahlias, michaelmas daisies and scarlet leaves and berries. Fountains of barley stood at each pew end and, splayed against the pulpit was a, now seldom seen, proper old-fashioned sheaf of wheat. That evening the church was packed to the doors and, later, so was the Parish Room where the farmers' wives catered for the annual Harvest Supper. I was numbered among the farmers' wives despite Gordon's habitual assertion that I was the farmer and he the farmer's husband.

We did not have a corn harvest at Westwath. The harvest for which we gave thanks was hay and calves and, for two never-to-be-forgotten years, lambs.

This season Butterscotch made her own modest contribution to the festival—a single kitten. He was the same pale creamy-beige shade as Meatpie, the butcher's kitten. It was a pretty colour and thinking he would be company for poor deaf Butter, we decided to keep him. Sadly his grandmother, Charlotte, had been a road victim some weeks earlier so he brought the cat population up to six again.

Thidwick (Roger happened to be reading a library book called *Thidwick, the Kind-hearted Moose*; the kitten, he declared, would be a kind-hearted mooser), being an only child, was the sole candidate for his mother's milk and expanded before our eyes. He had a tummy like a barrel and thighs like butter-tubs which was surprising considering he was never still for a couple of seconds together. Like most of us Fusseys, both feline and human, he had a nose of note ('Big noses,' Gordon often remarked, 'run in our family'), a circumstance which emphasized the deplorable truth that he never washed it. He was the grubbiest kitten I ever saw—a feline hippie if ever there was one and a source of great concern to his mother.

While too tiny to do otherwise he submitted to Butter's searching tongue but by the time he had reached the size of a large mouse he was already well on the way to delinquency. With a paw planted on his tum, Butter did her best to lick the other bits. Thidwick writhed and screamed, shouted that baths were weakening and did she want him to grow up a cissy? Working on the hypothesis that cleanliness was debilitating he argued that the opposite would make him strong and spent most of his waking hours upside down in the coke-hod, spinning around inside it like a reaming tool. We may have had the dirtiest kitten, but we possessed the cleanest coke-hod interior in the North Riding.

When he wasn't polishing up the kitchen scuttle he was in one or another of the open fireplaces in the living or dining rooms poking exploratory paws between the bars of the empty grates. We put a fire-guard around each, wedging them tightly to the stone facing with heavy iron ash-tidies and buttressing them with pokers, hearth-brushes and fire-tongs. The chimney flue exercised the same influence on Thidwick as Castle Farm did on the rest of our livestock. He flattened himself like a splash of cream and peered, saucer-eyed, upwards through the fire-screen mesh. One day when he was big, he promised us, he would climb right to the *top*.

He was just the right size, though, to crawl beneath the big, black iron turf plate and sit happily beside the ash-pan. From this refuge he would answer back his mother who peered anxiously underneath. Finally one of us would have to kneel on the hearthrug and haul him out covered with cinders and feeling ready to take on Big Daddy.

Instead of motherhood bringing contentment, poor Butterscotch went around looking more haunted than ever and her loud 'Oh, *Thid*wick' wail became a background sound as familiar as the ticking of a clock. It turned up, unfailingly, on every tape-recording we made.

We had only recently bought the recorder and were enthusiastically taping everything from Gordon singing to the cows, to teatime at Roger's birthday party. (What a boring occasion that must have been. Almost total silence highlighted only by a sudden shriek from somebody to the effect that her foot was stuck between the chair spells.) Butterscotch's dirge quite enlivened *that* recording but Delius would have a fit over 'La Calinda'. Another tape was completely ruined by what sounded like a bomb explosion in the quiet bit. What it *was* was Thidwick knocking the fire-irons for six.

Thidwick's hippie period lasted, perhaps, a couple of months, and then he suddenly reformed and washed himself fanatically, making loud snickering noises at the hardened bits until his coat was as beautiful as nature intended. Then, with the fervour of the newly converted, he set about his relations. It didn't please them much but we managed to tape a few decent recordings at last.

Following closely on the heels of the Harvest Festival came the annual village chrysanthemum show where, it really being not my year, I put my foot right in it. 'I don't like *that* one,' I said, unequivocally, to Mrs Horner standing next to me, about a rather cold-looking mauve.

'No?' she said after a rather long pause. 'It's ours.'

Life being what it is, she was nowhere in earshot when I

warmly praised a lovely cream one. The prize card, I noticed later, bore her husband's name.

A week or so after that episode we moved that blasted straw yet again. Well, some of it. About a hundred bales which we had packed in next to the generator shed beneath the Robin's Nest. This was not a good place to keep anything because it was right next to, and overlooking, the beck, a situation liable to reversal after heavy rain. During our first Westwath year we had lost a quantity of straw through flood action and had steered clear of that particular storage place ever since, but we *had* to put it there again because, dash it, there was simply nowhere else.

It was melting snow, this time, that drastically raised the water level. November snow on our hills is normal and we had had a week of it. It had arrived suddenly and ruthlessly, lengthening my morning work by an hour, trapping cars in drifts and sentencing our visiting Local History Lecturer to a homeward tramp over ten miles of blizzard-ridden moor road.

Not content with that the elements had to make a production of it. On Sunday morning we were awakened by thunder, lightning and a howling gale to find that although it was still snowing thinly, a thaw had set in and, encouraged by the disorderly atmosphere, fate set about flinging spanners in all directions.

First, I found the kitchen's Calor gas cylinder was empty. Rather than brave the weather and dark outside to fetch a new bottle I drew up the Rayburn to boil the kettle and made tea by the light of the hurricane lamp. Next, Robert was sick all over the clean washing airing in the bathroom, and Antony, testing the ice on the beck to see if it would still bear his weight, found it wouldn't.

The beck grew noisier with the ageing day. When we went out at evening milking time, light from the pressure lamp revealed racing black water level with the bank top and it was visibly rising every minute. A few inches more and it would be seeping through the dry stone wall and into

106

the straw.

It was positively the *last* time he was going to shift straw about like this, cried Gordon, as he had done for years. He would put up a proper building and it would be used only for straw. Did we hear him? *Only* for straw. If we didn't catch pneumonia after this lot he'd eat his hat!

If the four of us hadn't been sweating buckets I should have agreed with him, because we were all soaked to the skin. It wasn't merely the sleet that was responsible for this, or the number of times we had slipped and fallen in the slush, but our way led past a waterspout that kept following us about.

Water streaming down the hayshed roof into the guttering poured straight out of the open end because we hadn't got around to fixing a fall pipe. This was handy in the ordinary way because it kept the hens' drinking bowl topped up, but directed by the tempestuous wind it took on a manic life of its own and, like a hosepipe at full throttle, picked out each of us as, bale-laden, we skated past on water-covered ice.

It was like a lifesize game of snakes and ladders.

'If hit by waterspout, go back two paces,' cried Gordon, himself moving a few steps forward faster than intended.

As it happened we could have stayed comfortably indoors. The beck rose no higher. The ground beneath the Robin's Nest stayed dry as dust.

All that got wet was us, our clothes and, of course, the straw.

16

Come All Ye Faithful

In no time Christmas with its Fayres and Gift Stalls was upon us. Cupboards and drawers were ransacked for suitable donations. Owls and hanging plantpot-holders were macraméd, handkerchiefs embroidered, gloves and dishcloths knitted. Though not by me. My offering, I decided, would be something simple and non-time-consuming.

I gathered and dried graceful, droopy larch branches thickly clustered with cones. A quick spurt of gold and silver spray and I could get the job over in a couple of minutes. Best, though, to do it in the garden.

Outside the back door I laid newspapers on the paving-stones, spread out the branches, pulled the tops off the aerosols and began.

That was the signal for Thidwick and the two Bundies to catapult from the house, dive headlong into the news-papers and attack the larch sprays which, they said, started it first. Only Thidwick intercepted some of the glitter. This was when he was at the scruffy stage and he looked more like a punk rocker than ever.

I retrieved the branches, paper and aerosols and set them up again in the farmyard beyond the garden gate. Immediately I was mobbed by a crowd of muddy-footed hens who pecked critically at the larch cones, recognized them as those old things that fall from the sky and walked them muckily into the ground.

I salvaged the remains, hoping that some of the mud would be disguised by the paint, walked over the beck the long way round to put the cats off the trail, and slipped into the orchard by the big white wooden door. The sprays had, by this time, lost some of their grace. Not to mention bobbles.

I set up the bits of sticks under the yew tree and, with aerosol blazing furiously, tried to make up with glitter what they lacked in everything else; that was when Jess, hot on my scent and fortuitously coming across the bit of fallen wall where the wrought-iron gates were about to be hung, came suddenly upon me from behind.

Jess was the only dog in the parish that Christmas to have a golden halo around her head. Just like a Christmas angel, she said happily. Wasn't it *lucky* she'd found me?

That was also why the yew tree sported a gold-plated trunk and Robert's school's Christmas Fayre had bunches of fresh holly as my contribution that year.

That year, for the first time, we joined with a group of villagers to sing carols in aid of blind children. Gordon had quite a pleasant tenor voice: the boys and I couldn't sing for toffee as we would be the last to admit, but everyone was welcome and we added volume if nothing else. We couldn't meet them until Gordon returned from work so the waites were already on circuit when we drove into the village. We stopped by the common, wound down the windows and listened. The silence was tangible.

Frost glistened on the roadway and was reflected in the star-spangled sky. Mellow lighted windows of houses and cottages lay like a golden sediment in the dark bowl of surrounding moors. Far away, creeping up over the rim, a tiny light marked an anonymous vehicle on the lonely road to Whitby.

The church clock startlingly struck the hour and as if on cue, the door of the handsome creeper-clad hotel opposite opened wide, a broad golden band streamed across the green and with it the people we were searching for. We looked them over carefully but they were merely mellow with coffee, lemonade and crisps, generously exchanged in return for carols.

'Trust us to miss that,' grumbled Robert fitfully until cheered a few doors later by chocolates at the Vicarage and biscuits somewhere else. The biscuit people may have had an ulterior motive—it was a while before we could sing again—but most people were pleased to see us. Often doors stood wide long before we reached them. Some people shivered on their doorsteps and sang with us . . . others, where there was room, invited us inside.

We broke up at ten o'clock with freezing feet and, in the case of young Paul who had expertly played the mouth organ accompaniment all evening, freezing fingers. But we were warm inside.

Our village, though home to only three hundred or so souls, sprawls over many acres with lengthy walks between houses. Over the years we found that three crammed evenings were not long enough to call on everyone and the outliers, who were inevitably missed, never knew their luck.

That Christmas we had time for only one more evening. We began it at Moorend, an outpost of the village which is almost a separate community of its own.

It was an entirely different sort of night from the previous one. No frost or stars, only pitch darkness and an unremitting drizzle. Our way led through unlighted farmyards where one or two of our number thought they had been before. In daylight. In summer. Their memories of where paths lay were imaginative to say the least but very little manure got into our boots so we stood in reasonable comfort to sing our hearts out at cow byres and roofless out-houses.

However, there was an appreciative audience at the last farm along the lane. It was not the family, who—we learned later, long after we had rendered our speciality, 'Oh Come All Ye Faithful' and an extra verse of 'Once in

110

Royal David's City' because Paul accidentally started up again—were out winning prizes at the village whist-drive, but a flock of geese.

The geese had greeted us with the sort of enthusiasm that prompted me to push Gordon between them and me. Whether it was the influence of music, I couldn't say, but they gathered in a group with their heads together like the spokes of a wheel, and listened in enthralled silence. Either that or they were plotting our rout. We moved off sharply without proferring the collecting box, just in case.

Towards the inn, actually. We didn't go inside; there wouldn't have been room and it was past closing time. The inn is one of the tiniest in the country for all that its signboard was painted by a Royal Academician. We stood outside in the narrow, deserted roadway and gave of our best to its landlady, and to Miss Allen, who lived opposite.

The rain turned to a drumming downpour. Wet to the skin and much colder than we had been that earlier, frosty night, we stood up to our ankles in a stream which seemed to have its source actually beneath the last cottage. Perhaps—I'm sure I hoped—it was only an impermanent consequence of the rain. We directed our voices to the lighted window and sang through our repertoire. The youngest children huddled on the doorstep with the collecting boxes and rapped on the door at every verse end . . . all we wanted was to finish and go home to our beds.

Water poured noisily over the blocked guttering. Some of it which missed our collars gurgled loudly down a fall pipe. The stream flowed over our feet and bubbled into a conduit and rain hissed and thrummed—all in unfair competition with our voices. At last, as no one came to the door to put us out of our misery, we rounded off with our usual last chorus, one normally cheerfully rendered as thanks for donations received. This time we let it rip with feeling.

'We *wish* you a merry Christmas and a *happy* new year!'

The children thundered a final non-productive tattoo with

the door knocker and we turned to go—some people had already moved off into the blackness, their cries as they fell into gullies fading with increasing distance—when the door slowly opened. The elderly householder who had come out merely to fill his coal-bucket, nearly died of shock when he saw us. 'Whativer are you doing out theer, then? What? Carol singing? Whyiver didn't you knock?'

Singing again at the Carol Service in the warm, bright church we caught each other's eye and grinned reminiscently. Though I had nothing to smile about . . . I had been appointed to read a lesson and my legs had turned to jelly.

I had rehearsed the passage until I almost knew it by heart then at the last minute was having a duck-fit because I was suddenly convinced I was pronouncing some of the words wrongly.

Long before the service was due to start I was changed and ready. So, thanks to my jumpy condition, was the family. On tiptoes we picked our way across the muddy field to the garage with me threatening what I would do to them if they got any of it on their clothes, and settled ourselves in the car. It wouldn't start.

Gordon flung up the bonnet and did things with the plugs. The boys contributed unsolicited and venturesome advice and I sat in frozen silence with horrified eyes glued to my watch.

Brought up in a family to whom punctuality was of the essence it really pains me to be late. My father used to shepherd Mother and me to the station at least an hour before the train was due to leave and Scarborough annually welcomed us off a train that steamed out earlier than the one intended. I kept it up after I was married—couldn't help myself—and the boys and I spent more hours on draughty stations waiting to be picked up by friends who were expecting us after lunch than I care to remember. Since moving to Westwath holidays had ceased to be but I still worried.

Five minutes before the service was due to begin, Gordon was flinging tools about with increasing wildness, the boys

112

were risking their necks with every word they uttered and I raced back to the house to phone the Vicar's wife. I caught her just as she was about to cross the road to church.

Certainly she would read it for me if I didn't get there, she said, but she hoped I *would* as *her* knees had started knocking now. Wait—she knew what she'd do, she said with inspiration born of funk. She'd send someone down to pick me up.

Back at the garage with shoes more than a mite muddy, I shut my eyes to Gordon wiping filthy hands on something that was not old rag.

'Get in quick,' he said tersely.

'Somebody's coming . . .'

'*In!*'

As we leaped up the hill we passed Betty Smithson racing down. As we swung round the corner she was doing a tight U-turn.

We shushed each other through one doorway as the choir filed in through the other. They were singing 'Oh Come All Ye Faithful'. . .

I read the lesson. The roof didn't fall down or my hair drop out nor, to Robert's relief, did I show myself up in any way—the time I measured my length during the Dashing White Sergeant at a local hop Robert half expected we should have to leave the district—and we returned home full of Christmas joy and *bonhomie*. Before a great log fire we relaxed with neighbours who had called in. Gordon went up to the bathroom and didn't come back. Deep in conversation we didn't miss him until Robert returned from the same errand.

He paused in the doorway until he had our attention.

'Dad's back,' he announced dramatically, 'has Gone Again!'

17

To dream, perchance, of sleep

Gordon's back 'went' at unlikely moments and in inconvenient places. He could carry hundredweight sacks of dairy nuts two at a time without giving it a passing thought, hoist up and fit solid stone gateposts weighing goodness knows how much without feeling a twinge, but he only had to pick up an envelope off the floor to lock himself in intimate and prolonged communion with chairlegs, or stoop over the car boot to find himself on his knees in the snow before being brought home on a stretcher.

Because of his back, Gordon always slept flat out on a board at night and for the rest of that Christmas he was confined to it by day as well.

When he was up again he could move about only in one rigid piece like an agonized tailor's dummy which was why, a week later, he was gliding round the fields like a Dalek at the head of a procession consisting of Robert with wheelbarrow full of manure, me with spade, fork, bucket of bonemeal and twenty-four oak saplings, Jess with bone and thoughtful expression and Storky, Dark Bundy and Thidwick with nothing other than pure and simple nosiness.

We were planting, we told Binnie, Joan Arrowsmith and the Calor gas man, for posterity.

There were already a lot of trees at Westwath. A heck of a lot too many, we thought at times. Particularly in autumn as we hurriedly swept the leaves off the steep cart-track so that the coalman could get his lorry out again, and scraped sopping dollops out of roof guttering while water cascaded down and inside windows. But there had been a number of fatalities over the past few years, one way or another—victims of flood and old age. Only the previous autumn, prompted by the sudden shedding of a hefty lower limb on to the footbridge a moment after he had stepped off it, Gordon had sawn down a long-dead, soaring spruce tree. It had stood at the bottom of the garden, and how to fell it while causing the least damage was something that gave him a headache for days. Not, however, such a headache as he would have had if he'd stayed on the bridge a second or two longer.

It ought to have been child's play to him because when he was younger and we lived in town he, single-handed, had felled a fully-grown elm with a handsaw. He had had to judge that to a fraction. A yard or so too far to the left and it would have demolished a neighbour's garden. A yard or so too far to the right would have meant curtains of the wrong sort for the other half of our semi. And had it gone backwards . . . well, prefabs weren't supposed to be as temporary as all *that* . . . For the record—it came down in sections entirely in our own small plot just in time for the local kids to drag away the thinner branches and brushwood for Guy Fawkes night bonfires. I know the effort involved because guess who was at the other end of the cross-cut saw slicing up the recumbent yard-thick bole?

There was more room to play about in this time. Nevertheless, it was with the very familiar feeling of wishing myself elsewhere that I gripped the end of a guide rope. The other end, after passing through a series of pulley blocks attached to other trees, was fastened around the spruce. At the opposite side of the garden Robert and

Antony were similarly stationed. Mother and Roger, safely indoors, washed their hands of it altogether.

Gordon had already cut a wedge out of the nearer side of the tree—nearer to me, that is. He pulled the starter cord of the chainsaw and began the second cut. As the blade bit into the wood and the roar of the saw increased so did my conviction that I ought to have been moved to a place of safety along with the other valuables.

Gordon had most solicitously shifted the stone sundial out of harm's way. Getting on for its second century, he said. Mustn't damage it, must we?

Also in a place of safety he had deposited a rather nice concrete stone vase made by my father many years ago. Didn't want to hurt that, either, he had said. He had moved it, I suddenly recalled vividly, from a spot only a yard or so from where I clung sweatily to my rope. I had a good mind to go over and discuss it with him but at that moment the tree creaked, cracked, smashed and tumbled just where Gordon said it would—diagonally across the whole width of the garden with its head resting on the hayfield steps. The firewood in that just about lasted through the winter.

We were doing a lot of planting for posterity that winter but, unfortunately, posterity will see very little of it. There were no willows weeping into the beck so, lovingly, I planted some. The cows eliminated those in their second summer. I replaced them with suckers of white poplar that had been given to us. The beck rose suddenly one night and washed away the riverbank, poplars and all. Those oak trees which, under Gordon's directions, I planted around our boundaries with barrowloads of compost, manure, bone meal and muscle-fatigue, were wiped out in a single afternoon by the Forestry Commission clearing *their* boundaries while, apparently, under the impression that self-sown acorns had done remarkably well that year.

I was hopping mad but Gordon, who never bothered to lose his temper, planted a smacking kiss on my cheek. 'Never mind, love,' he said. 'As one door shuts another closes.' This was a favourite saying of his and, with us, only

116

too true. Jess and the cats shrugged it off, too. It had all been a waste of good holes, anyway.

Not that there weren't compensations. We had our minor successes. Magazines were beginning to accept a few articles I had written and Gordon was awarded ten pounds—to us a fabulous sum—for high marks in the Ford Registered Technician scheme. That was a feather in his cap as the scheme for Ford employees was nationwide and award winners relatively few.

By the end of the month Gordon's back had improved enough for us to turn our energies to work indoors. But even that was a rehash of earlier industry.

I don't know why the bedrooms seemed always in need of drastic rearrangement. Or perhaps I do. In the first place we possessed so many beds, what with three of Mother's, three of our own, one inherited with the house and another which was a hand-me-down from a friend. All these beds—and only three bedrooms and an attic to put them in.

In the second place we had never been straight since the hectic two-houses-into-one move at the beginning of our life at Westwath when almost immediately the main room had been requisitioned by paying guests. In the confusion chests had lost their partners and wardrobes rubbed shoulders with alien beds.

None of us, except Mother, had put down taproots but had slept in each and every bed in turn, and for some weeks, while the house was undergoing repairs, Gordon and I even had to lodge in the bungalow.

From the beginning Mother had occupied a single bed in the small back room but had, we were concerned to learn, been secretly pining for her old double bed all the time.

'Why not,' said Gordon, 'swop the beds, sort out the rest of the stuff and let Mother have her own suite to herself again?'

One reason why not was because the room wasn't big enough. We turned the bed on its side, upended it, twisted it forty-five degrees and set it down again. That gave us a

117

whole extra twelve inches to play about with but there was not enough room for the larger of Mother's two wardrobes, compress it as we might. We shuffled the wardrobe back on to the landing and on into the boys' room where there were two others already. One of these was Mother's small one. This fitted exactly into her room and would even open its doors so long as the bedroom door was shut. And *that* would close if the kneehole dressing-table, dragged from the main bedroom, was wedged at an eccentric angle across the opposite corner. That left the bedside table which *would* have gone in provided that none of the other doors or drawers ever opened again. Mother cheerfully dispensed with that.

She felt much happier now, she said, surrounded by her own belongings. Besieged, I thought, would be a better word.

The single bed spurned by Mother replaced Roger's cot and joined two others in the boys' room . . . after one of the wardrobes and the long elegant dressing-table had been manhandled out of it and into our big room . . . which already contained two double beds and a chest of drawers. The chest of drawers was not a matching member but was antique and roomy and, as it stuck in the doorway anyway, we let it stay.

By nightfall there was hardly an item of furniture in its original position. At last everything was stationed where we wanted it. Even the double bed from the attic had replaced a shabby one in the bungalow (three beds in there, too!) leaving on the attic floor a single mattress of undulating contour which no one recalled ever having seen before and which was promised to the boys for their next bonfire.

So it was inevitable that one awful night a few weeks later Gordon and I were trying to sleep on it.

In our own room, occupying a double bed apiece, were friends of ours, mother and daughter. Unthinkingly, I had presumed that they would share a bed, and had intended borrowing the mattress of the other one for our use in the attic. I had left it too late. Isobel and Emily arrived earlier than expected, quite naturally believed they had a bed each and staked out their claim.

On the floor above in our eyrie under the eaves, Gordon and I spent a restless night. This blasted mattress, said Gordon, was so awful that it was even making corrugations in his back board. Poor Gordon, when he wasn't writhing in agony on his back he was recklessly crying he could stand no more of it, sitting up and fetching his head a crack on the rafters. Eventually, presumably knocked senseless, he rolled out altogether and spent the rest of the night flat out on the carpet.

Next morning we were greeted by our fresh and smiling friends. They *had* slept well, said Isobel contentedly. They thought it was the country air. Did we find it did the same for us?

Most people told us the same thing, I said, carefully evading the question. Painfully picking up the milking pail I crept shakily to the cowhouse.

That night we waited until Isobel and Emily had retired. Swearing that he was so tired he could sleep on a clothes-line—a claim he often made but never substantiated—Gordon swept cushions off chairs and settees, thrust some of them into my arms and quietly opened the stairs door. Simultaneously another door-latch clicked upstairs.

I was *sorry*. I didn't *mean* to hop back on to his toes, I whispered irritably. The secrecy was making me jumpy.

At all costs our sleeping arrangements must be kept from our guests. What if one of them was coming downstairs? Panic-stricken I began industriously thumping the cushions into place, uncomfortably aware that that in itself would be a suspicious circumstance if Isobel found me doing it. I have no reputation as a cushion-plumper.

Footsteps returning to the room above sounded the all-clear. Though slightly hysterical we reached the attic undetected and laid out the beds. The hysteria was less frivolous next morning. The cushions had been only marginally better than the mattress. Set side by side like a draughts-board they had formed a satisfactory-looking pallet but, as the night dragged on, tended to separate into their component sections. We discussed it for most of the night and by the small hours had reached general agreement that it was hips and elbows that bore the punishment this time. The sitting-room was put to rights long before Isobel and Emily appeared that day.

The following night I had all the cushions to myself while Gordon arranged some of his six-foot length on Roger's old cot mattress supplemented by a bolster. A fortnight of this and he would be a cripple for life, Gordon said. I mentioned the clothes-line but he ignored me.

With three sleepless nights behind me I leaped with eagerness at Joan Arrowsmith's offer of the loan of a feather bed.

Joan had laughed until she cried when, haggard-eyed, I had related my tale. How Gordon was getting through his work, I couldn't imagine, I told her. I myself was a walking zombie.

Gordon's eyes took on a yearning look when I told him about the feather bed. He would have driven over for it straightaway if we hadn't just then discovered that young Basher Bill, a red Hereford, had jumped a partition and was visiting the comely heifer next door. By the time that was dealt with—both pens mucked out to lower the floor and Basher reinstalled in his own quarters—it was almost ten o'clock at night and Joan was helpless again imagining us waiting until our guests had retired before we dare creep out.

Actually they were still downstairs when we crept back which was why we chose to use the side door.

There is a lot of weight in a good feather bed. This one was wrapped in a linen sheet and bound with binder twine and looked and felt like a large seaman rolled in his hammock and about to be buried at sea. One at either end, and not for the first time glad that we were invisible from the main road, Gordon and I shuffled in a crouching position beneath the sitting-room window round to the farther side of the house. The door was locked.

In the kitchen, Antony for the umpteenth time was reading his way through the whole Arthur Ransome series so was not at all taken aback when in true Swallows and Amazons style I tapped gently on the window and in dumb show indicated that he should secretly unfasten the dining-room door. The next move, hauling the thing upstairs without attracting attention—especially now that Antony was in on it and offering to do his bit by causing a disturbance to draw their fire—was tricky. At the other side of the door Isobel and Emily were laughing with Roger who should have been in bed but, due to an oversight on my part, wasn't. What they would have thought if they had opened the door and seen us preparing for a committal to the sea we shall never know because at that moment Roger threw a lucky tantrum and we scraped up the staircase unspotted.

That night we lay in comfort. Next morning Binnie phoned to express the hope that Judith's twenty-first birthday party hadn't kept us awake.

No, we told her truthfully but jadedly, it hadn't. It was the seventy-five-strong car rally doing a Starsky and Hutch round the corner that *had*.

18

Alarm call

We all have our problems. Will Arrowsmith's was a blockage in his land drains. He told me about it while we awaited our turn in the mobile bank that visits the village twice a week.

Dug up half the field, they had, and did I know what it was?

I was mystified and said so.

'A moose-wezzle,' said Will triumphantly.

'Merciful heavens!' I exclaimed and nearly fell backwards off the bus.

I still don't know what a moose-wezzle is. I asked Joan and she didn't know either. Neither of us can remember to ask Will.

We stumbled into someone else's bad patch on Saturday lunchtime a few days later. We were disembarking from the car by our garage when we were accosted by a harassed-looking young man who asked us if we had passed a party of young people up the road? We had seen no group answering to his description. As we talked it dawned on me that his face, as well as looking harassed, was also familiar. He was, I accused him, Leslie Parkin, a one-time member of Gordon's scout troop in a village near Hull!

Prompted, he recognized us too. This naturally brought on a spate of reminiscing which continued until Leslie remembered his missing party. He was now a Youth Leader, he explained, and had brought a vanload of youngsters out for a trip to the sea, breaking the journey in order to enjoy a short country ramble. *They*, he said, had hoped for a long walk over the moor but he had vetoed this because, one, there wasn't time and, two, they weren't equipped for it.

He had compromised by dropping them off up-river by the Youth Hostel, instructing them to follow the beck to the hamlet of Moorend where he would leave the van and walk along the beck the opposite way to meet them. This latter reach is not a walk but a difficult scramble yet here he was having completed it, emerging on to the road by the stile near the bridge, with never a sign of the kids.

Sticking to the beck, he said, he had believed it impossible to get lost!

Ah, but, we told him, he hadn't done his homework. Because, although in places there was a well-trodden path, this was made by Matt Stewart's cattle and was not a public right of way. Even so, had the youngsters bumped into Matt and been turned out on to the moor it would have made no appreciable difference to their walk. They would only have to follow the wall which ran roughly parallel with the beck and should have reached this point long ago. Our guess was that they were still in the vicinity of the hostel where there were interesting places to lark about in.

We all agreed how jolly it had been to see each other after all these years and separated, Leslie to go on towards the hostel, we to our lunch and afternoon work. Now he knew where we lived, we called after him, we hoped it wouldn't be so long before he visited us again.

It was exactly three hours as it turned out. He was standing at our back door no longer merely harassed but downright frantic. Not only had his charges vanished into thin air but when he had enquired at Ghyll House and Rowan Head Farms he had earned rocketings for encouraging—albeit innocently—trespass.

The weather had been dull and depressing to start with

123

and what had begun as a blurring of the landscape had developed into mist. In the absence of any contrary evidence Leslie had convinced himself that, like ships in the night, their courses had somehow crossed and he had returned to the van at Moorend fully expecting the youngsters to be waiting there. They weren't, of course, and once more he had fetched up at Westwath toiling the hard way along the beck. He was tied in knots trying to be in half a dozen places at once. He simply couldn't understand why such a simple outing could go so wrong.

He had our deepest sympathy. It was the sort of thing, we told him, that happened to us all the time and if he was prepared to risk our being involved we should be glad to do what we could to help.

Gordon reversed the car out of the garage and ran Leslie back to Moorend. He was going to wait hopefully by the van while we searched all roads by car. We would rendezvous, said Gordon, at four-thirty but, first, we would synchronize our watches. In Leslie's case it was a watch. In ours, it was the bedroom alarm clock... our watches both being out of commission, it had to be that or the Westminster chimes.

We began by driving along the road that led to the hostel, meeting no one but sheep. Up there, at the higher reaches of the beck, was a convergence of streams. It seemed unlikely, but was just possible, that the children had followed the wrong one *up*-river. They could be miles away in the wrong direction now. Gordon turned the car and drove along the road that swung in a great arc to cross the broadest of these streams high up on the moor.

There, it was as desolate as only a heather moor out of season can be. The general charcoal greyness of the immediate foreground merged quickly into milky white where the afternoon's gauzy mists had drawn together becoming thicker and woollier every minute. The narrow road bored through the fog, shooting-butts and occasional standing-stones along its borders looming in high relief like cardboard cut-outs as we passed them. Two or three times Gordon stopped the car, switching off the engine, to listen. The moisture-laden air struck chill through the lowered windows. It was the sort of day best spent before a warm fire or, at the worst, well wrapped in waterproof clothing and wearing strong boots. Leslie's party, prepared only for an hour or so by the sea, were clad in light jackets and shoes, good enough for the comparatively easy walk he had allowed them but certainly not adequate for this.

The road kinked and dipped. A group of trees materialized from the back-cloth and we heard the musical sound of water. We had reached the ford across the stream. Gordon halted the car and we stepped out on to the sheep-mown grass.

To our surprise, there was a car already parked there. On the river bank, heedless of the weather, a young couple stood with arms around each other's waists. Through the cold swirling mist they were gazing into one another's eyes while water dripping from the trees made dark patches on their shoulders. We thought they were nuts.

Without much confidence, in the circumstances, in their powers of observation, we enquired if they had come across a party of young people who may have seemed lost.

They looked at us with blank faces. In particular they looked oddly at me. Definitely touched, poor things, I thought, as we turned back to the car. At that moment the alarm clock in my hand exploded into sound, the tintinnabulation sounding shocking in the cottonwool silence. Startled, I glanced back at the young couple. They were staring after us, their faces completely expression-less... It wouldn't have been so bad if they'd *said* something.

'Honestly,' I said as we drove hurriedly away,' *they* must have thought *we* were mad... Carrying a bedroom alarm clock around with us. And the thing to actually go *off*...' That was the galling part, because we never set the alarm in the general way. I always woke without it.

I should think myself lucky, Gordon said cheeringly. It *could* have been the Westminster chimes.

Back at Moorend Leslie was doing handsprings. He went to the little pub and phoned the police. Gordon dropped me off at home and went on with the search alone. A short while later Leslie in the van drew up outside.

He had had a message from the police. The blighters had turned up in a village four miles away having done what he'd expressly forbidden, walked overland across the moor. They hadn't even attempted to follow the beck...

I was relieved. They could have died of exposure out there.

'They are very lucky,' I began, 'to get to the village...'

'They would have been luckier,' said Leslie grimly, 'if they hadn't...' And on that menacing note he drove furiously away.

Back in our kitchen Binnie, whose bizarre and numerous tribulations were second only to ours, was having a cup of tea with Mother. We talked over the afternoon's events.

'I bet he was furious,' said Binnie. 'He must have been worried sick. I tell you what, though,' she went on with a sort of surprised satisfaction. 'It makes a change it happening to somebody else... not to you or us.'

And she went home to find that the water cistern in their loft had split asunder, its contents seeping with maximum effect through the bedroom ceiling.

19

Goodbye my Bluebell

It was a comfortable feeling knowing that none of those troubles was ours. What *we* had were disintegrating vehicles, non-thriving calves (well, one— the French Faggot, and serve her right), a barren cow, Robert with bronchitis and Antony just being himself.

Antony was going through a phase. On his thread of life he had blithely strung phases like gradated pearls, each becoming more impressive as it moved farther away from that doubtful time around one midnight in May eleven years before, when he made his first appearance on earth. The time was so doubtful that none of us, doctor, nurse or myself, knew for certain whether he was Sunday or Monday's child. We took a vote and plumped for Sunday. It is this awful insecurity, I expect, which is responsible for his individuality. Accident-prone he had always been. Hospital casualty doors hardly ever stopped swinging for him. Cuts were routine, concussion commonplace and his latest misfortune was to become the innocent victim of a young thug on the school train. His face was a technicolour mess. It was hardly surprising, therefore, that somewhere along life's path he had lost his memory as well. But it was aggravating for the rest of us.

Few messages entrusted to Antony arrived at their destinations. Out-of-date school notices turned up as unreadable crumpled balls in the laundry. I learned about Open Days an hour before they were due to begin when kind souls with transport phoned to offer me a lift. You name it, Antony could forget it. The nadir was reached one day when he was sent home from school early because of bad weather conditions. He arrived home soaked to the skin because he had forgotten to put on his coat and boots... this, knowing he had to walk a mile of blizzard-swept moorland road with snow up to his knees. Also he had left behind his lunchbox and, making a thorough job of it, had forgotten to give Pauline—who was in Robert's form—a note to pass on to their form master explaining Robert's absence. Honestly, I felt beleaguered.

Even Robert seemed infected with absent-mindedness. He hadn't been seen since lunchtime, when we thought about it. He wasn't around at teatime and didn't turn up when called for. Mother, for one, thought that very ominous and worried about it. Robert, for all he never put on an ounce of surplus flesh, always enjoyed his meals. At school, he read the dinner menu not as three choices but as a programme and worked his way through the lot, so Mother's fears were not without foundation.

Gordon had been making new doors for calfpens most of the day and had not seen anything of him. My last glimpse of him had caught him aimlessly circling the yard on his bike. Antony wasn't at home. He had gone up to Castle Farm early in the afternoon and had stayed there for tea.

'That's it,' I said. 'He'll have gone up to Castle Farm on his bike. He'll be all right.'

'Aren't you going to give them a ring to make sure?' said Mother anxiously, visualizing him simultaneously dead in a ditch, drowned in the beck and five miles from home with a flat tyre.

'Oh, we'll give him a bit longer,' I said carelessly. I stepped outside and yelled his name a few times in various directions. There *was* an answer but it was from the French Faggot yodelling in the dark like an echo and effectively drowning out any other possible reply.

At eight o'clock, just to please Mother, I phoned the Arrowsmiths knowing full well that Robert was there watching television by a roaring fire.

He wasn't. Immediately, to mother's list of disasters, I added another. Lying at the bottom of the ravine with a broken leg. At *least*.

By this time even Gordon was looking thoughtful. After all it was pitch dark. Robert had been missing a long time and he hadn't told us he was going anywhere.

He *hadn't* gone anywhere. Or, anyway, no farther than the garage. All the time we had been shouting and speculating he had been lost to the world in the intricacies of an old motor he had dismantled, working in Arctic conditions by the ungenerous glow of an oil lamp. When Gordon shone a torch into the gloom Robert's jaw dropped with surprise.

Yes, of course he'd been there all the time. No, he hadn't heard us shouting. Well yes, he was a bit cold now we mentioned it, and he *was* hungry. We hadn't had our *tea*, had we?

We were just closing the garage door when Pauline and Antony arrived full of excitement and readiness to form a search party. They were terribly disappointed to see Robert.

'You've *found* him,' said Pauline accusingly.

'Oh, *heck*,' seconded Antony, seeing a heroic rescue ignominiously dissolving into the ether. The possibility of Robert lying battered and bleeding at the bottom of the ravine obviously had had a different effect on them.

And that is how Robert got bronchitis.

But our saddest time was to come. Bluebell was sixteen years old and had borne thirteen calves. The thirteenth was to be her last. Never had she looked so fit. Her eyes were bright, her coat shone and she came regularly and enthusiastically into season at three-weekly intervals. The AI man wore a track to the door. So did the vet when it became increasingly obvious that something was amiss.

'Cysts on the ovary,' pronounced Mr Burn. He could

remove them but they would probably grow again. After all, the old lady was getting on a bit...

The cysts did return. Refusing to accept the inevitable we called in the vet again. And again.

Mr Burn shook his head. 'You know, it's no good,' he said at last. 'She'll never get in calf again. Send her away.'

We were shattered. Westwath without Bluebell was unthinkable. If we could have afforded it there is no doubt we should have kept her on in honourable retirement to the end of her natural life. But it was impossible. We could barely afford to keep ourselves.

Cravenly I didn't see her go. I plugged my ears so I shouldn't hear the cattle-waggon labouring away up the hill.

Set faced, Gordon returned to the house and put his arms around me. I soaked his jersey with tears. 'She wasn't frightened, was she?' I asked despairingly. I couldn't bear her to be frightened. Fright, I believe, is much, much worse than pain.

'Bluebell?' scoffed Gordon, in a desperate attempt to be cheerful. 'Not she!' She had been a bit doubtful at first, he said, but as soon as she saw the two Hereford bullocks looking down at her from the waggon she marched straight up the ramp and jostled them. *She* was boss-cow around here, she had told them. And they'd better not forget it.

I forced a watery smile and wept for a fortnight.

The animal element was well to the fore just then. Only a few days after Blue's departure Heather produced her first calf for us. She did it at half past ten on the very morning she was due, with no fuss, no histrionics and no disowning of the baby. Calmly and competently she took charge of the new little heifer, drying it off with a rasping tongue and relaxedly letting down her milk when I guided the soft muzzle to the udder.

Neither was there any milk fever nor any complications whatsoever. I could hardly believe it. Indeed, the only excitement occurred when Rhoda accidentally caught her horn under the strap of my coat sleeve, hoisting my wrist high in the air, and we stuck there, eyeball to surprised eyeball until I could persuade her to lower her head and release me.

Peace in the cowhouse did not mean that life had become humdrum however. In other spheres there were odd goings on. For one thing a suitor had come to call on Jess. He had appeared unannounced early in the morning before she was up and sung a passionate serenade outside the dog-house door. Awakened from sleep, we didn't enjoy it. Jess did and with uplifted voice turned the thing into a duet.

It was more than we could stand. We dressed and went outside. Romeo's howls never faltered as we fumbled around his neck in search of a collar. He hadn't one. With no means of identifying him we just hoped he would go away.

To our relief he did. Gordon departed for work and I milked cows, fed calves and worked my way through the usual morning jobs. I had attended to the stock in the top field and was climbing back over the gate when the dog appeared again. I shouted and waved the empty bucket at it.

Ernie Miller was driving past from the direction of the village. He couldn't see the dog. He could see nobody but me sitting on a gate waving a bucket. He gave me a nervous smile and hesitantly waved back. Well, my first wave hadn't been intended for him so generously I gave him a vigorous one for himself. He put his foot on the accelerator and vanished over the bridge.

Pat, the postman, arrived at that moment. A regular visitor to all the farms in the district he, I hoped, might recognize the dog. I wasn't surprised when he didn't—one mongrel sheepdog is very like another—but he helped create peace by holding on to the stranger who, I must say, was very cooperative, while I let Jess out of the dog-house, ran with her to the kitchen and shut her inside. Then we shoved her young man into the dog-house and shut the door behind him. An hour or so later his owner—Matt

Stewart, as it happened—came in search of him.

But I was still not free of trespassers ... not by a long chalk. A tell-tale bleating drew me to the road. Four sheep were grazing the verge by our top gate. Jess held them in a mesmerized knot while I toiled uphill to the cattle grid and opened the gate wide. Then, obeying my whistle, she drove them through it and onwards a quarter of a mile for good measure while I contributed the usual shouted remarks.

Back home I collected hammer, nails and binder twine and set out on a tour of our boundaries. The fence between the Browns' house and the cattle grid still clung tenuously to life. I went on through the grid on to the moor and examined the length of the top field wall. It still stood to its full height, its swags of wool-decorated barbed wire intact. Before retracing my steps I stood for a while looking through the leafless trees down the steep quarry-like face at the cold grey beck purling around the rocks. Down again at the bottom of the hill I glanced up to the field I had left only moments before. There were four sheep calmly grazing there. Inventing new and better curses I scrambled over the gate and wrathfully flung the hammer in their direction. Ernie Miller, driving home wouldn't see the sheep who were now over the top of the hill. All he saw was me astride the gate brandishing a hammer.

Wearily I dropped to the ground. There could be hardly a soul in the neighbourhood by now who did not think me demented.

A few seconds later I almost was. The garage field was holding an At Home for another contented party of old ewes.

I didn't entirely swallow my scream. I *knew* they couldn't get in through the roadside fence. I *knew* they hadn't come over the top field wall. I hoped—oh my, how I *hoped*—they hadn't climbed up the Scar ... I had had a hair-raising day fencing that lot last year.

They hadn't. They had waded under the road bridge where the swollen beck had washed the sheep netting away, and had scrambled up the bank on our side and into

132

the field. The clue to that was the classic one. The sandy shore was thickly pock-marked with hoof prints. I was going to have to take a closer look at that cold grey water right then.

Gordon's wellingtons came higher up the leg than mine so I went home and swopped them. Size ten, they were, and felt every bit of it. In them I clumped back to the bridge, the original hammer, nails and binder twine supplemented by a couple of lengths of useful-looking wood and pockets full of staples. I climbed the stile and slid down the muddy bank into the water. The sheep netting had not entirely gone, I found. The force of the current had prised it from its fastenings at the farther side and had swung it under the nearside bank where, well buried in sand, it dragged heavily at its moorings. Tugging wouldn't budge it. I galumphed back home for the spade.

By the time I had released the wire and fought off its advances I hardly noticed the temperature of the water. I was even glad of the chill when, ages later, I had scrambled up the bank, climbed over the stile, trudged across the bridge, climbed over *that* fence and slid down the opposite bank—repeating the whole sequence in reverse order—about a dozen times. Because, to get the netting across the bridge aperture, first I had to attach one end of a ball of binder twine to the end of the netting, throw the ball across to the other bank, then pull in the twine and haul the netting over.

Now I admit that I'm a rotten shot but even when the ball didn't fall short or tangle in the hazel bush behind me but landed fair and square on the opposite side, by the time I had completed the obstacle course in one direction, the teasing water had pulled it back and carried it off again before my hand could make contact with it.

I won at last and secured the wire to its bolts. The lengths of wood were rammed in for rigidity, and thorn bushes packed between them and the dank, mossy bridge walls. The walls magnified and echoed water noises and overhead occasional traffic rumbled. Once, also overhead, over the parapet of the bridge a trilby'd head appeared, jumped like a faun when it saw me, and vanished. I jumped, too, but was grateful that the head belonged to a stranger and not, for instance, Ernie Miller.

Ernie Miller passed when the job was completed and I was up on the top of the stile threatening with the spade a couple of ewes that had strolled up to criticize my handiwork.

Thanks to the intervening parapet of the bridge, he couldn't see the sheep.

20

Technical hitch

While my troubles leaned heavily towards the animal, Gordon's afflictions tended to be chiefly of a mechanical nature. On three mornings in succession he had had difficulty in starting the car. On the evening of the third day he came home very late indeed.

'Cylinder block cracked,' he reported despondently. He had stayed behind to work on it, driving home at last in a car belonging to the firm. The following night he appeared in yet another vehicle—an estate car this time—and from the rear he dragged out a small cultivating machine.

Good old Don had lent us it, he said. To dig the potato patch with, he went on informatively on seeing my rather blank expression.

I had made a wild guess and come up with that. I was only surprised, I explained, because borrowing was something we seldom indulged in.

He hadn't borrowed it, Gordon said patiently. Don had *lent* it to us. If I tried very hard I could just detect the difference.

At the weekend, he promised, he would dig in the whole of that couch grass once and for all. Well chopped up and buried deeply it would give us no more trouble.

My heart lifted. Our land was light and, where clear of weeds, easy to dig, but that wickens-infested piece had defied all my labours. Scruples melted and vanished. I had a wonderful vision of that cultivator turning my life into a bed of roses.

What it actually did was hammer another spike into Gordon's bed of nails because with the first reverberation of the motor the handle came off in his hand and he had to set up his equipment to weld it back on again. Then, hardly had he turned off the gas cylinders and restarted the motor than the connecting rod snapped in two. So, before it was even started, digging was suspended until a few weeks later when a new rod could be bought and fixed, by which time it was too late to plant potatoes anyway.

In the meantime, Gordon went on repairing our car and on those evenings, instead of getting off the school train at the usual stop, Robert stayed on and travelled right up the line to the station nearest his father's place of employment. Helping Gordon with all his breakdowns was good training for a would-be apprentice mechanic.

They were having far too many late nights. I checked the clock with the radio and confirmed that it really was eleven o'clock again.

'Do you know it's eleven o'clock *again*?' I said sternly to the opening back door.

'Is it, love?' said Gordon unrepentantly, enfolding me in a bear-like hug which brought a lot of cold outside air with it. 'We had a breakdown.'

I stepped back with a tearing sound. Gordon's coat had a Velcro fastener and in crowded shops he stuck to perfect strangers. They would waltz round between the counters chest to chest, Gordon politely doffing his hat and his partner thinking she was being molested.

'Another breakdown?'

'Another *other* breakdown.' He sounded completely unruffled.

'The breakdown vehicle broke down,' said Robert, adding to the confusion.

'What breakdown vehicle?'

'Dad has bought another Morris Traveller,' said Robert,

'and we were towing it home.'

I was getting out of my depth. I took a deep breath. 'We've *got* a Traveller,' I said carefully, 'that doesn't go. Why do we need another one that apparently doesn't go either? And how much did you pay for it, for goodness sake?'

'Give us a kiss,' said Gordon sultrily.

'Fifteen pounds,' said Robert. 'And we've got it for spare parts. But the Transit broke down on Easton bank and we were stuck there in the dark with the blue light flashing. Then Mr Arrowsmith came and rescued us.'

'*Who* came?' I yelped.

Gordon flopped into a chair and covered his eyes with one hand in the tradition of Sir Henry Irving. 'There we were,'—his voice was charged with emotion—'blue light flashing like a frost-bitten lighthouse ... ACCIDENT printed in large letters across both sides. Miles from home ... and who should turn up but Will.' He paused to let the enormity sink in. It did. The number of times Will has come to our aid right on cue is remarkable.

Honestly, Gordon sighed, he felt like pulling his cap down over his face and pretending it wasn't him.

Will, running in a new engine, had only chanced to drive that way. 'Lucky, wasn't it?' he had said, and brought the pair of them home.

Next morning, in pouring rain, Gordon returned to the stranded Transit on his bike. There he met one of his workmates who had brought another vehicle. With it they towed the Traveller home and left it on the roadside verge by the Scar field gate. Then they returned to the Transit and towed that in the opposite direction back to the garage. Breaking down—would I believe it, said Gordon, wearily that night—on the way.

That was their worry. Mine was what the neighbours would think when they saw what was gracing our gateway. Already it had drawn a knot of interested calves.

Ecologically speaking it was no asset. It did not appear to have an engine ... in fact hardly any front at all. One of the doors was off its hinges and leaned casually against the body, and a wheel was missing. Stuffed inside and bristling out all over were five good bales of hay.

It would have been a pity to waste the space, Gordon said.

It had been a long cold winter and spring was late. For all we had begun the season with masses of hay there was, by then, very little left and Gordon had bought a few bales from a farm near the garage.

That weekend I begged, for his first job, that Gordon should fetch the eye-sore down into the yard and decently hide it from public view.

Gordon was hurt . . . he had a soft spot for Travellers. He said it wasn't an eye-sore. He said it was beautiful.

In the theory, 'there is beauty in the bellow of the blast' he may have had a point.

To my surprise the neighbours' comments were favourable ones. They had believed we had parked the thing up there deliberately to store hay in and thought it a splendid idea.

'Slovenly lot,' said Gordon primly. 'Fancy having neighbours like that!'

Still we hadn't finished with car trouble. Shortly after the last episode we were in the thick of it again.

Unexpectedly, friends we hadn't seen for ages dropped in. They were taking a short break in a beauty-spot village a few miles away and called on us one afternoon while Gordon was at work. He was so disappointed at having missed them that, when he arrived home, nothing would satisfy him but that he would turn around and go and visit *them*, this despite the car being dangerously low on petrol. Will power, we gathered, could do anything. Will power undoubtedly did.

Robert and I accompanied him. It was shortly after we turned off the main road that other facts began to emerge. The first was that the car had lost all its gears except the one we were currently using. The second was that the handbrake had become non-functional.

The road—to call it a secondary one would be ostentatious—after threading a humble and decorous course through the heather for a number of miles, suddenly lost its head and plunged downhill, swerved madly, dropped down through a water splash and went up the other side like an arrow. The car, in its single gear, did all these things, too, and had just recovered from its surprise when the whole sequence occurred all over again.

Being an utterly conventional person myself, a non-driver and a great respecter of the law, I sat in frozen horror waiting for the engine to drop out or a police patrol to pounce out of the heather. Neither happened. A few world-weary sheep were the only creatures to note our passing.

It was dusk when we reached our destination. The garage where Gordon had confidently expected to refuel was closed and Joan and Bob, who can't have known us so well after all and were not expecting us, were not at home. We walked around and up and down the sprawling hilly village peering fruitlessly into lighted hotel bars until it was quite late. And dark.

That was when Gordon disclosed another of the car's defects. The battery, he told us cheerfully, was flat.

By this time the fuel gauge was registering several degrees below zero. When it didn't respond to thumping Gordon airily said it had always been a wicked pessimist, threatened the engine until it coughed weakly into life and, accepting the dictatorship of the second gear, started us off on the homeward trail.

Like the fuel gauge, I was convinced we should never make it. As the crow flies, we were roughly seven miles from home. The road, circumventing a huge forest, covered almost three times that distance.

Wishing to know just how long a walk lay ahead of us, I searched the toffee-paper compartment and found a large-scale Ordnance Survey map. Maddeningly, for a third of the way, the road actually led *away* from home. 'Looking-glass Land,' I said bitterly and hoped the petrol would run out *now* where we could take a short cut through the forest. A second or two later, with the footpath behind us, I was praying that it wouldn't.

The road turned the corner at the bottom and started on a course parallel with home. At each likely-looking short cut I half rose from my seat, only, once it had fallen away on the port quarter, to flop back again and will us on to the next one. To save fuel and battery we coasted lightless downhill becoming legal only when we approached the two small villages en route.

Robert, full of advice and instructions, leaned over from the back seat like the Farndale Hob. (Come, you *must* have heard of the Farndale Hob? He was the malevolent sprite who had billeted himself on a family living in a remote cottage in Farndale—a piece of scenery situated only a few miles from where we were at that moment. The family blamed him for their child's illness, crops failing and stock succumbing to all the things stock habitually succumb to (A syndrome not unfamiliar to us, now that I considered it.) At last they could stand it no longer. They piled their belongings on a cart that hadn't collapsed with woodworm, harnessed the horse—which must have been immune to hobs—and fled into the night. On the way they met a neighbour who asked what they were doing.

'We's flittin',' chorused the family.

'Aye,' echoed the Hob from the rear of the cart. 'We's flittin'.'

Robert was just like that. An idea took root. In the light of it I turned in my seat and examined him suspiciously. He looked solid enough.

We saw no one until we reached Spode, the second village. A young woman was coming out of a cottage. I nearly slid off my seat in astonishment.

Spode is a funny place. Sometimes it's there and sometimes it isn't. On the occasions when it is there, there is never, under any circumstances, anybody in it.

The first time I encountered it I was on a short Youth Hostelling holiday with a friend. We had walked miles

140

through dense forest, eventually emerging on to a long lonely road so were pleased when, at last, a desultory scattering of cottages began to appear around us. Spode was having one of its on days. Hoping for directions, we knocked on doors. Not a lot of doors because there weren't many cottages, nevertheless we pounded on every door there was. Almost without exception these doors stood open and somnolent sheepdogs lay across the thresholds. There was not a human being in the place. And never had been on all the times we had passed through since.

We have pondered long over this phenomenon because the village possesses a well-known silver band and its members must be recruited from somewhere . . . next time I must look to see if the conductor's baton has a star on its tip.

The young woman disappeared into the night and normality reigned. Robert gave it as his opinion that, to help reduce the population explosion, people should be taken to Spode where they would be absorbed and vanish . . .

Behind us Spode retired to its particular etheric plane and, at last, we were pointing in the right direction for home on a section of road surface that wouldn't be tolerated on the moon. We climbed over the dark empty moor, dropped to where water glinted, lifted again and approached the end of the tractor track which led down to Rowan Head, the Phillipses' farm. Only a mile, if we had to walk that way, to home. My spirits rose for all of ten seconds. Or it might have been eleven. Six miles of road still lay ahead.

All at once an unnatural calm flowed over me. I stopped worrying. What was to be, would be . . . jail or death from exposure . . . it was all the same to me. Still unmoved I said nothing when, a hundred yards from the junction with the main road, the car was beaten by a sudden sharp contour and the engine threw in its hand. I sat quiescent and peaceful while Gordon and Robert hauled a spare battery from the boot and, using jump leads, goaded the long-

141

suffering engine to new life.

We coasted round the corner past darkened Castle Farm where Will peacefully slumbered, and came to a standstill on our own dear patch.

'Shall I,' I enquired of Gordon innocently, as I opened the back door, 'phone Will and tell him, it's all right, we've managed?'

P S

In April that year technology took an enormous step forward. The astronauts returned safely from the moon and at Westwath fertilizer- and muck-spreaders came on the strength. The spreaders weren't quite new. Gordon had paid thirteen pounds for the two of them at an implement sale. Christopher Phillips had also bought a muck-spreader at the same sale and the pair of them spent most of the day towing the purchases home at five miles per hour. I had, I hoped, tossed my last shower of fertilizer pellets by hearth shovel out of a bucket, and flung my last forkful of manure.

The hover-mower was brand new, though. With it I was going to tame the unpaved part of the terrace garden and create new lawns along the beck beyond the house. With garden ideas teeming through my head and out of my fingers I could hardly wait to begin.

On the livestock side things were looking up, too. All but the Charolais and an under-age friend of hers had been passed with flying colours by the Min. of Ag. inspector, and even the French Faggot was looking better after a vitamin injection.

Old friends, Bluebell and Rosie, were no longer around to annoy and amuse us, but they would always be remembered with extra-special affection as Snowdrop and

Sarah, the new generation, grew up to take their place. Left alone in the Scar field when the bullocks were sent to market, they had called loudly after the retreating cattle-waggon. It was sexual discrimination again, they yelled. If the boys were going for a nice ride why couldn't they go, too? Their indignant voices were augmented by others floating up from the farmyard . . . the bleat of a tiny calf bought only that day . . . Heather bellowing because, mistakenly, she thought it was hers . . . Charolais bawling because she was mentally deficient, and her young Angus friend roaring just for the hell of it.

Away up on the skyline in the Scar field, strolling along under the length of the electric fence, her raised tail only fractionally short of it, Light Bundy pretended she was a trolley-bus.

In short, all was well, and mechanically and animalwise we looked set for a rosy future.

Which only goes to show that as well as Joan and Bob, Mr Cardew and Gordon, *I* didn't know us very well, either.